About the author

Samuel Langhorne Clemens (alias Mark Twain) was born in Florida, Missouri in 1835. He spent an idyllic childhood in the town of Hannibal on the banks of the Mississippi. At 12, after his father's death, he was apprenticed to a printer and soon began to take an interest in writing. At 22 he trained and served as a river-boat pilot. After a brief period as a Confederate irregular during the Civil War he headed west to try his luck prospecting for silver. It was out west that he turned to journalism serving his time on newspapers in Nevada and California where he first used the pseudonym 'Mark Twain' (a river pilot's measurement of depth). He shot to national celebrity in 1865 with the publication of his 'Jumping Frog' story and never looked back, becoming one of the greatest and most prolific figures in American letters, crowning his career with his masterpiece *The Adventures of Huckleberry Finn* (1885). Having made and lost several fortunes, he died in 1910.

Cannibalism in the Cars

THE BEST OF TWAIN'S HUMOROUS SKETCHES

Prion Humour Classics

Mapp and Lucia	E F Benson
How Steeple Sinderby Wanderers Won the FA Cup	J L Carr
The Diary of a Provincial Lady *	E M Delafield
The Papers of A J Wentworth, BA	H F Ellis
Squire Haggard's Journal	Michael Green
The Diary of a Nobody	George and Weedon Grossmith
Three Men in a Boat	Jerome K Jerome
Mrs Caudle's Curtain Lectures	Douglas Jerrold
Sunshine Sketches of a Little Town	Stephen Leacock
No Mother To Guide Her	Anita Loos
The Serial *	Cyra McFadden
The World of S J Perelman *	S J Perelman
The Education of Hyman Kaplan *	Leo Rosten
The Return of Hyman Kaplan *	Leo Rosten
The Unrest Cure and other Tales	Saki
My Life and Hard Times *	James Thurber
Cannibalism in the Cars	Mark Twain

* for copyright reasons these titles are not available in the USA or Canada in the Prion edition.

Cannibalism in the Cars

THE BEST OF TWAIN'S HUMOROUS SKETCHES

MARK TWAIN

with a new introduction by

ROY BLOUNT JR

PRION

This collection published in 2000 by
Prion Books Limited,
Imperial Works,
Perren Street,
London NW5 3ED

ISBN 1-85375-369-6

Jacket design by Keenan
Jacket image courtesy of British Library
Printed and bound in Great Britain
by Creative Print & Design, Wales

Contents

INTRODUCTION

by ROY BLOUNT JR

In an interview, Oliver Stone, the movie director, condescends to praise another director's heavy-handed baseball comedy for "telling a story in a big, broad, Mark Twain kind of way". No. If anyone's way of telling a story is big and broad, or anyway broad, it is Oliver Stone's. Mark Twain is still funny, ninety years after his death, because his way was fine.

You might say that a man's claiming to have been shot nine times, beaten with a cowhide whip, stripped nearly naked, scalped, hit by a brick through the window, thrown through the window himself, and injured by shrapnel from a stove exploded by a hand grenade on his only day at a Tennessee newspaper is a broad way of depicting journalism in that state. But consider this bit of dialogue:

"Sir, have I the honor of addressing the poltroon who edits this mangy sheet?"

"You have. Be seated, sir. Be careful of the chair, one of its legs is gone. I believe I have the honor of addressing the putrid liar, Col. Blatherskite Tecumseh?"

"Right, sir...If you are at leisure we will begin."

"I have an article on the 'Encouraging Progress of Moral and Intellectual Development in America' to finish, but there is no hurry. Begin."

Then, as one gentleman to another, they start blazing away in each other's general direction with large pistols, in the process thrice clipping the narrator. "I then said, I believed I would go out and take a walk, as this was a private matter, and I had a delicacy about participating in it further. But both gentlemen begged me to keep my seat, and assured me that I was not in the way."

If this is broad, it is broad as Monty Python is broad, not as Benny Hill. There is in fact a Python sketch in which starving mariners argue over which of them should be eaten by the others—the captain is offended when none of the crew regards him as toothsome; they settle on making a stock of him. The Python sketch is deft, all right, but Twain's "Cannibalism in the Cars" is at least as amusing, is sustained longer, and offers more (I venture to say, though I have never belonged to the Royal Navy) in the way of verisimilitude.

You could call it broad for a man to complain that his watch, after a repairer of watches worked on it, performed as follows: "For half a day it would go like the very mischief, and keep up such a barking and wheezing, and whooping and sneezing and snorting, that I could not hear myself think for the disturbance; and as long as it held out there was not a watch in the land that stood any chance against it. But the rest of the day it would keep on slowing down and fooling along until all the clocks it had left behind caught up again." The watch "averaged well", but this "is only a mild virtue in a watch". If this is broad, it is broad as Borges is broad, in the original.

You might harbor the stereotypical notion that any sort of glass-eye humor, on the face of it, is broad. But glass-eye humor that crops up naturally in the course of things, as it does in "His Grandfather's Old Ram" ("She was a good soul—had a glass eye and used to lend it to old Miss Wagner, that hadn't any, to receive company in; it warn't big enough.…She could never tell when it hopped out, being blind on that side, you see. So somebody would have to hunch her and say, 'Your game eye has fetched loose, Miss Wagner dear'") and keeps on calmly topping itself without ever undermining Miss Wagner's aplomb—I don't call that fine, because fine is too broad a term. I call that delicate.

Not broad, then, are Mark Twain's distinctive effects. Nor, except in the ripples they continue to make, are they big. Although he may have come closer than anyone else to writing the Great American Novel, Twain is not a master at book length. The Mississippi River is big and broad, and so is the issue of American slavery, but *The Adventures of Huckleberry Finn*, in which Huck travels down that river with a runaway slave, is distinguished not by sweep or cumulative power, but by moments, episodes, bits of dialogue or description and, most importantly, a boy's narrative voice.

Like Twain the first-person humorist, Huck Finn the first-person moralist is absolutely straight-faced. I was going to say "adventurer" instead of "moralist", but Huck is not seeking adventure, he is trying to do the right thing—and trying, to be sure, to find a little personal freedom, but not out of a sense of entitlement. He feels guilty about being unable to tolerate conventional strictures. Similarly, Twain's own persona in his sketches is not looking for humor, he is just trying to get by and keep normal time in a crazy world. Bowing out of bloodthirsty Tennessee journalism, he does not claim the moral high ground. He informs his editor, "I like you, and I like your calm unruffled way of explaining things to the customers; but you see I am not used to it ....Southern hospitality is too lavish with the stranger."

Huck is an unreliable narrator in that he never quite sees things the way the reader does, but his taking outrageous comic rapscallions at face value makes those characters all the more comic, just as his judging himself a dark sinner for going good-heartedly against established mores makes the enormity of those mores clear without sermonizing. By something like the same token, Twain is a salubriously unreliable essayist. His way is matter-of-fact, which enables him to go surreal as if against his will. His way is plain speaking, which enables him to be set upon by wonderfully resounding and tawdry rhetoric. If he had his way, life would be simple, peaceful, unfunny. No barber would have "made a handle of my nose, to assist him in shaving the corners of my upper lip, and it was by this bit of circumstantial evidence that I discovered that a part of his duties in the shop was to clean the kerosene lamps."

You don't leave as many epigrams and celebrated paragraphs to posterity as Mark Twain did ("It is by the goodness of God that in our country we have those three unspeakably precious things: freedom of speech, freedom of conscience, and the prudence never to practice either of them") by being big and broad. The American humorists who came before him were heavy on dialect and have not worn well. Twain blended various strains of American vernacular into a fluid narrative mode that has influenced not only later humorists such as James Thurber and Garrison Keillor but also later novelists such as Ernest Hemingway (who said that modern American literature began with *Huckleberry Finn*) and Saul Bellow.

His great books of travel and reminiscence (including *Roughing It*, from which some of the pieces in this collection are taken) are large misshapen affairs cobbled together of wonderful highlights (and padding). He made his name in the first place by means of comic sketches. In the mid-1860s he wrote a number of them for daily and weekly newspapers in California and Nevada (whence he had traveled after giving up the Civil War as not his sort of affair). Other periodicals around the American states and territories circulated these early *jeux d'esprit* widely, and respected literary papers in New York began to welcome his contributions. "The Celebrated Jumping Frog of Calaveras County," which appeared in the New York *Saturday Press* in November of 1865 (under a slightly different title), created a sensation. A rough frontier tale, in its matter, but its texture is exquisite, an extraordinary weft of empathy and detachment. He couldn't make a living out of short freelance humor (who, alas, has ever been able to?), so he turned his hand to books and lecturing, thereby becoming a major writer and a beloved public character. But he continued to write sketches throughout his career. The best of these, along with *Huckleberry Finn*, are the works of his that are most read today.

Mark Twain enjoyed coming off as an old gold-miner, a failed one at that, but his style was lapidary. He might rather have been describing his own style when he wrote of his friend William Dean Howells, "He seems to be almost always able to find that elusive and shifty grain of gold, the right word. Others...are miners working with the gold-pan—of necessity some of the gold washes over and escapes; whereas, in my fancy, he is quicksilver raiding down a riffle—no grain of metal stands much chance of eluding him....A powerful agent is the right word; it lights the reader's way and makes it plain; a close approximation to it will answer, and much traveling is done in a well-enough fashion by its help, but we do not welcome it and applaud it and rejoice in it as we do when the right one blazes out on us. Whenever we come upon one of those intensely right words in a book or a newspaper the resulting effect is physical as well as spiritual, and electrically prompt; it tingles exquisitely around through the walls of the mouth and tastes as tart and crisp and good as the autumn-butter that creams the sumac-berry."

Howells is not widely read anymore. Few people today could tell you how a sumac-berry tastes, or precisely what mining process is alluded to in "quicksilver raiding down a riffle". But as long as any form of written English is intelligible to anyone, I'll wager, the best bits of Mark Twain will persist in being "electrically prompt".

Editor's Note

All but the final five sketches in this collection were written and published in the years between 1863 and 1872. They represent Twain's literary apprenticeship and the purest expression of the irreverent, vernacular humour that was the very soul of his genius. Twain first started writing having fallen on hard times while prospecting for silver in Nevada. He was asked to contribute to the *Virginia City Territorial Enterprise* in 1862 after sending the paper a number of humorous letters, written for his own amusement and signed 'Josh'. The sketches in this collection have been arranged in chronological order by the year of there first appearance in a daily or weekly newspaper: most notably, the *Californian*, *Galaxy* and the *Buffalo Express* (which Twain both edited and had a financial interest in). Three of the pieces are not newspaper sketches at all but stand-alone yarns from Twain's fictionalised Western memoir *Roughing It* (1872). The stories were often syndicated and once they had been collected in book form: *The Celebrated Jumping Frog of Calaveras County, and Other Sketches* (1867) and *Sketches New and Old* (1875), they became hugely popular and frequently pirated on both sides of the Atlantic. There are several versions of many of Twain's newspaper sketches, he often rewrote and re-edited them. We have endevoured to reset from the earliest available sources and retain the original variant spelling and punctuation wherever possible.

AG

Curing a Cold

IT is a good thing, perhaps, to write for the amusement of the public, but it is a far higher and nobler thing to write for their instruction, their profit, their actual and tangible benefit. The latter is the sole object of this article. If it prove the means of restoring to health one solitary sufferer among my race, of lighting up once more the fire of hope and joy in his faded eyes, of bringing back to his dead heart again the quick, generous impulses of other days, I shall be amply rewarded for my labor; my soul will be permeated with the sacred delight a Christian feels when he has done a good, unselfish deed.

Having led a pure and blameless life, I am justified in believing that no man who knows me will reject the suggestions I am about to make, out of fear that I am trying to deceive him. Let the public do itself the honor to read my experience in doctoring a cold, as herein set forth, and then follow in my footsteps.

When the White House was burned in Virginia, I lost my home, my happiness, my constitution, and my trunk. The loss of the two first-named articles was a matter of no great consequence, since a home without a mother or a sister, or a distant young female relative in it, to remind you, by putting your soiled linen out of sight and taking your boots down off the mantle-piece, that there are those who think about you and care for you, is easily obtained. And I cared nothing for the loss of my happiness, because, not being a poet, it could not be possible that melancholy would abide with me long.

But to lose a good constitution and a better trunk were serious misfortunes.

On the day of the fire my constitution succumbed to a severe cold caused by undue exertion in getting ready to do something. I suffered to no purpose, too, because the plan I was figuring at for the extinguishing of the fire was so elaborate that I never got it completed until the middle of the following week.

The first time I began to sneeze, a friend told me to go and bathe my feet in hot water and go to bed. I did so. Shortly afterward, another friend advised me to get up and take a cold shower-bath. I did that also. Within the hour, another friend assured me that it was policy to "feed a cold and starve a fever." I had both. So I thought it best to fill myself up for the cold, and then keep dark and let the fever starve awhile.

In a case of this kind, I seldom do things by halves; I ate pretty heartily; I conferred my custom upon a stranger who had just opened his restaurant that morning; he waited near me in respectful silence until I had finished feeding my cold, when he inquired if the people about Virginia were much afflicted with colds? I told him I thought they were. He then went out and took in his sign. I started down toward the office, and on the way encountered another bosom friend, who told me that a quart of salt water, taken warm, would come as near curing a cold as any thing in the world. I hardly thought I had room for it, but I tried it any how. The result was surprising. I believe I threw up my immortal soul.

Now, as I am giving my experience only for the benefit of those who are troubled with the distemper I am writing about, I feel that they will see the propriety of my cautioning them against following such portions of it as proved inefficient with me, and acting upon this conviction, I warn them against warm salt water. It may be a good enough remedy, but I think it is too severe. If I had another cold in the head, and there were no course left me but to take either an earthquake or a quart of warm salt water, I would take my chances on the earthquake.

After the storm which had been raging in my stomach had subsided, and no more good Samaritans happening along, I went on borrowing handkerchiefs again and blowing them to atoms, as had been my custom in the early stages of my cold, until I came across a lady who had just arrived from over the plains, and who said she had lived in a part of the country where doctors were scarce, and had from necessity acquired considerable skill in the treatment of simple "family complaints." I knew she must have had much experience, for she appeared to be a hundred and fifty years old.

She mixed a decoction composed of molasses, aqua fortis, turpentine, and various other drugs, and instructed me to take a wine-glass full of it every fifteen minutes. I never took but one dose; that was enough; it robbed me of all moral principle, and awoke every unworthy impulse of my nature. Under its malign influence my brain conceived miracles of meanness, but my hands were too feeble to execute them; at that time, had it not been that my strength had surrendered to a succession of assaults from infallible remedies for my cold, I am satisfied that I would have tried to rob the graveyard.

Like most other people I often feel mean, and act accordingly; but until I took that medicine I had never reveled in such supernatural depravity and felt proud of it. At the end of two days I was ready to go to doctoring again. I took a few more unfailing remedies, and finally drove my cold from my head to my lungs.

I got to coughing incessantly, and my voice fell below zero; I conversed in a thundering bass, two octaves below my natural tone; I could only compass my regular nightly repose by coughing myself down to a state of utter exhaustion, and then the moment I began to talk in my sleep, my discordant voice woke me up again.

My case grew more and more serious every day. Plain gin was recommended; I took it. Then gin and molasses; I took that also. Then gin and onions; I added the onions, and took all three. I detected no particular result, however, except that I had acquired a breath like a buzzard's.

I found I had to travel for my health. I went to Lake Bigler with my reportorial comrade, Wilson. It is gratifying to me to reflect that we traveled in considerable style; we went in the Pioneer coach, and my friend took all his baggage with him, consisting of two excellent silk handkerchiefs and a daguerreotype of his grandmother. We sailed and hunted and fished and danced all day, and I doctored my cough all night. By managing in this way, I made out to improve every hour in the twenty-four. But my disease continued to grow worse.

A sheet-bath was recommended. I had never refused a remedy yet, and it seemed poor policy to commence then; therefore I determined to take a sheet-bath, notwithstanding I had no idea what sort of arrangement it was.

It was administered at midnight, and the weather was very frosty. My breast and back were bared, and a sheet (there appeared to be a thousand yards of it) soaked in ice-water was wound around me until I resembled a swab for a Columbiad.

It is a cruel expedient. When the chilly rag touches one's warm flesh, it makes him start with sudden violence and gasp for breath just as men do in the death agony. It froze the marrow in my bones and stopped the beating of my heart. I thought my time had come.

Young Wilson said the circumstance reminded him of an anecdote about a negro who was being baptized, and who slipped from the parson's grasp, and came near being drowned. He floundered around, though, and finally rose up out of the water considerably strangled and furiously angry, and started ashore at once, spouting water like a whale, and remarking, with great asperity, that "One o' dese days some gen'lman's nigger gwyne to git killed wid jes' such dam foolishness as dis!"

Never take a sheet-bath—never. Next to meeting a lady acquaintance, who, for reasons best known to herself, don't see you when she looks at you, and don't know you when she does see you, it is the most uncomfortable thing in the world.

But, as I was saying, when the sheet-bath failed to cure my cough, a lady friend recommended the application of a mustard plaster to my breast. I believe that would have cured me effectually, if it had not been for young Wilson. When I went to bed, I put my mustard plaster—which was a very gorgeous one, eighteen inches square—where I could reach it when I was ready for it. But young Wilson got hungry in the night, and ate it up. I never saw any body have such an appetite; I am confident that lunatic would have eaten me if I had been healthy.

After sojourning a week at Lake Bigler, I went to Steamboat Springs, and beside the steam baths, I took a lot of the vilest medicines that were ever concocted. They would have cured me, but I had to go back to Virginia, where, notwithstanding the variety of new remedies I absorbed every day, I managed to aggravate my disease by carelessness and undue exposure.

I finally concluded to visit San Francisco, and the first day I got there, a lady at the Lick House told me to drink a quart of whisky every twenty-four hours, and a friend at the Occidental recommended precisely the same course. Each advised me to take a quart; that made half a gallon. I did it, and still live.

Now, with the kindest motives in the world, I offer for the consideration of consumptive patients the variegated course of treatment I have lately gone through. Let them try it; if it don't cure them, it can't more than kill them.

1863

Aurelia's Unfortunate Young Man

THE facts in the following case come to me by letter from a young lady who lives in the beautiful city of San José; she is perfectly unknown to me, and simply signs herself "Aurelia Maria," which may possibly be a fictitious name. But no matter, the poor girl is almost heart-broken by the misfortunes she has undergone, and so confused by the conflicting counsels of misguided friends and insidious enemies, that she does not know what course to pursue in order to extricate herself from the web of difficulties in which she seems almost hopelessly involved. In this dilemma she turns to me for help, and supplicates for my guidance and instruction with a moving eloquence that would touch the heart of a statue. Hear her sad story:

She says that when she was sixteen years old she met and loved, with all the devotion of a passionate nature; a young man from New-Jersey, named Williamson Breckinridge Caruthers, who was some six years her senior. They were engaged, with the free consent of their friends and relatives, and for a time it seemed as if their career was destined to be characterized by an immunity from sorrow beyond the usual lot of humanity. But at last the tide of fortune turned; young Caruthers became infected with small-pox of the most virulent type, and when he recovered from his illness, his face was pitted like a waffle-mould and his comeliness gone forever. Aurelia thought to break off the engagement at first, but pity for her unfortunate lover caused her to postpone the marriage-day for a season, and give him another trial.

The very day before the wedding was to have taken place, Breckinridge, while absorbed in watching the flight of a balloon, walked into a well and fractured one of his legs, and it had to be taken off above the knee. Again Aurelia was moved to break the engagement, but again love triumphed, and she set the day forward and gave him another chance to reform.

And again misfortune overtook the unhappy youth. He lost one arm by the premature discharge of a Fourth-of-July cannon, and within three months he got the other pulled out by a carding-machine. Aurelia's heart was almost crushed by these latter calamities. She could not but be deeply grieved to see her lover passing from her by piecemeal, feeling, as she did, that he could not last forever under this disastrous process of reduction, yet knowing of no way to stop its dreadful career, and in her tearful despair she almost regretted, like brokers who hold on and lose, that she had not taken him at first, before he had suffered such an alarming depreciation. Still, her brave soul bore her up, and she resolved to bear with her friend's unnatural disposition yet a little longer.

Again the wedding-day approached, and again disappointment overshadowed it: Caruthers fell ill with the erysipelas, and lost the use of one of his eyes entirely. The friends and relatives of the bride, considering that she had already put up with more than could reasonably be expected of her, now came forward and insisted that the match should be broken off; but after wavering awhile, Aurelia, with a generous spirit which did her credit, said she had reflected calmly upon the matter, and could not discover that Breckinridge was to blame.

So she extended the time once more, and he broke his other leg.

It was a sad day for the poor girl when she saw the surgeons reverently bearing away the sack whose uses she had learned by previous experience, and her heart told her the bitter truth that some more of her lover was gone. She felt that the field of her affections was growing more and more circumscribed every day, but once more she frowned down her relatives and renewed her betrothal.

Shortly before the time set for the nuptials another disaster occurred. There was but one man scalped by the Owens River Indians last year. That man was Williamson Breckinridge Caruthers, of New-Jersey. He was hurrying home with happiness in his heart, when he lost his hair forever, and in that hour of bitterness he almost cursed the mistaken mercy that had spared his head.

At last Aurelia is in serious perplexity as to what she ought to do. She still loves her Breckinridge, she writes, with true womanly feeling—she still loves what is left of him—but her parents are bitterly opposed to the match, because he has no property and is disabled from working, and she has not sufficient means to support both comfortably. "Now, what should she do?" she asks with painful and anxious solicitude.

It is a delicate question; it is one which involves the lifelong happiness of a woman, and that of nearly two thirds of a man, and I feel that it would be assuming too great a responsibility to do more than make a mere suggestion in the case. How would it do to build to him? If Aurelia can afford the expense, let her furnish her mutilated lover with wooden arms and wooden legs, and a glass eye and a wig, and give him another show; give him ninety days, without grace, and if he does not break his neck in the mean time, marry him and take the chances. It does not seem to me that there is much risk, any way, Aurelia, because if he sticks to his infernal propensity for damaging himself every time he sees a good opportunity, his next experiment is bound to finish him, and then you are all right, you know, married or single. If married, the wooden legs and such other valuables as he may possess, revert to the widow, and you see you sustain no actual loss save the cherished fragment of a noble but most unfortunate husband, who honestly strove to do right, but whose extraordinary instincts were against him. Try it, Maria! I have thought the matter over carefully and well, and it is the only chance I see for you. It would have been a happy conceit on the part of Caruthers if he had started with his neck and broken that first; but since he has seen fit to choose a different policy and string himself out as long as possible, I do not think we ought to upbraid him for it if he has enjoyed it. We must do the best we can under the circumstances, and try not to feel exasperated at him.

1864

A Touching Story of George Washington's Boyhood

IF it please your neighbor to break the sacred calm of night with the snorting of an unholy trombone, it is your duty to put up with his wretched music and your privilege to pity him for the unhappy instinct that moves him to delight in such discordant sounds. I did not always think thus: this consideration for musical amateurs was born of certain disagreeable personal experiences that once followed the development of a like instinct in myself. Now this infidel over the way, who is learning to play on the trombone, and the slowness of whose progress is almost miraculous, goes on with his harrowing work every night, uncursed by me, but tenderly pitied. Ten years ago, for the same offense, I would have set fire to his house. At that time I was a prey to an amateur violinist for two or three weeks, and the sufferings I endured at his hands are inconceivable. He played "Old Dan Tucker," and he never played any thing else; but he performed that so badly that he could throw me into fits with it if I were awake, or into a nightmare if I were asleep. As long as he confined himself to "Dan Tucker," though, I bore with him and abstained from violence; but when he projected a fresh outrage, and tried to do "Sweet Home," I went over and burnt him out. My next assailant was a wretch who felt a call to play the clarionet. He only played the scale, however, with his distressing instrument, and I let him run the length of his tether, also; but finally, when he branched out into a ghastly tune, I felt my reason deserting me under the exquisite torture, and I sallied forth and burnt him out likewise. During the next two years I burned out an amateur cornet player, a bugler, a bassoon-sophomore, and a barbarian whose talents ran in the base-drum line.

I would certainly have scorched this trombone man if he had moved into my neighborhood in those days. But as I said before, I leave him to his own destruction now, because I have had experience as an amateur myself, and I feel nothing but compassion for that kind of people. Besides, I have learned that there lies dormant in the souls of all men a penchant for some particular musical instrument, and an unsuspected yearning to learn to play on it, that are bound to wake up and demand attention some day. Therefore, you who rail at such as disturb your slumbers with unsuccessful and demoralizing attempts to subjugate a fiddle, beware! for sooner or later your own time will come. It is customary and popular to curse these amateurs when they wrench you out of a pleasant dream at night with a peculiarly diabolical note; but seeing that we are all made alike, and must all develop a distorted talent for music in the fullness of time, it is not right. I am charitable to my trombone maniac; in a moment of inspiration he fetches a snort, sometimes, that brings me to a sitting posture in bed, broad awake and weltering in a cold perspiration. Perhaps my first thought is, that there has been an earthquake; perhaps I hear the trombone, and my next thought is, that suicide and the silence of the grave would be a happy release from this nightly agony; perhaps the old instinct comes strong upon me to go after my matches; but my first cool, collected thought is, that the trombone man's destiny is upon him, and he is working it out in suffering and tribulation; and I banish from me the unworthy instinct that would prompt me to burn him out.

After a long immunity from the dreadful insanity that moves a man to become a musician in defiance of the will of God that he should confine himself to sawing wood, I finally fell a victim to the instrument they call the accordeon. At this day I hate that contrivance as fervently as any man can, but at the time I speak of I suddenly acquired a disgusting and idolatrous affection for it. I got one of powerful capacity, and learned to play "Auld Lang Syne" on it. It seems to me, now, that I must have been gifted with a sort of inspiration to be enabled, in the state of ignorance in which I then was, to select out of the whole range of musical composition the one solitary tune that sounds vilest and most distressing on the accordeon. I do not suppose there is another tune in the world with which I could have inflicted so much anguish upon my race as I did with that one during my short musical career.

After I had been playing "Lang Syne" about a week, I had the vanity to think I could improve the original melody, and I set about adding some little flourishes and variations to it, but with rather indifferent success, I suppose, as it brought my landlady into my presence with an expression about her of being opposed to such desperate enterprises. Said she, "Do you know any other tune but that, Mr. Twain?" I told her, meekly, that

I did not. "Well, then," said she, "stick to it just as it is; don't put any variations to it, because it's rough enough on the boarders the way it is now."

The fact is, it was something more than simply "rough enough" on them; it was altogether too rough; half of them left, and the other half would have followed, but Mrs. Jones saved them by discharging me from the premises.

I only staid one night at my next lodging-house. Mrs. Smith was after me early in the morning. She said, "You can go, sir; I don't want you here; I have had one of your kind before—a poor lunatic, that played the banjo and danced breakdowns, and jarred the glass all out of the windows. You kept me awake all night, and if you was to do it again, I'd take and mash that thing over your head!" I could see that this woman took no delight in music, and I moved to Mrs. Brown's.

For three nights in succession I gave my new neighbors "Auld Lang Syne," plain and unadulterated, save by a few discords that rather improved the general effect than otherwise. But the very first time I tried the variations the boarders mutinied. I never did find any body that would stand those variations. I was very well satisfied with my efforts in that house, however, and I left it without any regrets; I drove one boarder as mad as a March hare, and another one tried to scalp his mother. I reflected, though, that if I could only have been allowed to give this latter just one more touch of the variations, he would have finished the old woman.

I went to board at Mrs. Murphy's, an Italian lady of many excellent qualities. The very first time I struck up the variations, a haggard, care-worn, cadaverous old man walked into my room and stood beaming upon me a smile of ineffable happiness. Then he placed his hand upon my head, and looking devoutly aloft, he said with feeling unction, and in a voice trembling with emotion, "God bless you, young man! God bless you! for you have done that for me which is beyond all praise. For years I have suffered from an incurable disease, and knowing my doom was sealed and that I must die, I have striven with all my power to resign myself to my fate, but in vain—the love of life was too strong within me. But Heaven bless you, my benefactor! for since I heard you play that tune and those variations, I do not want to live any longer—I am entirely resigned—I am willing to die—in fact, I am anxious to die." And then the old man fell upon my neck and wept a flood of happy tears. I was surprised at these things; but I could not help feeling a little proud at what I had done, nor could I help giving the old gentleman a parting blast in the way of some peculiarly lacerating variations as he went out at the door. They doubled him up like a jack-knife, and the next time he left his bed of pain and suffering he was all right, in a metallic coffin.

My passion for the accordeon finally spent itself and died out, and I was glad when I found myself free from its unwholesome influence. While the fever was upon me, I was a living, breathing calamity wherever I went, and desolation and disaster followed in my wake. I bred discord in families, I crushed the spirits of the light-hearted, I drove the melancholy to despair, I hurried invalids to premature dissolution, and I fear me I disturbed the very dead in their graves. I did incalculable harm, and inflicted untold suffering upon my race with my execrable music; and yet to atone for it all, I did but one single blessed act, in making that weary old man willing to go to his long home.

Still, I derived some little benefit from that accordeon; for while I continued to practice on it, I never had to pay any board—landlords were always willing to compromise, on my leaving before the month was up.

Now, I had two objects in view in writing the foregoing, one of which was to try and reconcile people to those poor unfortunates who feel that they have a genius for music, and who drive their neighbors crazy every night in trying to develop and cultivate it; and the other was to introduce an admirable story about Little George Washington, who could Not Lie, and the Cherry-Tree—or the Apple-Tree—I have forgotten now which, although it was told me only yesterday. And writing such a long and elaborate introductory has caused me to forget the story itself; but it was very touching.

1864

Advice for Good Little Girls

GOOD little girls ought not to make mouths at their teachers for every trifling offense. This kind of retaliation should only be resorted to under peculiarly aggravating circumstances.

If you have nothing but a rag doll stuffed with saw-dust, while one of your more fortunate little playmates has a costly china one, you should treat her with a show of kindness, nevertheless. And you ought not to attempt to make a forcible swap with her unless your conscience would justify you in it, and you know you are able to do it.

You ought never to take your little brother's "chawing-gum" away from him by main force; it is better to rope him in with the promise of the first two dollars and a half you find floating down the river on a grindstone. In the artless simplicity natural to his time of life, he will regard it as a perfectly fair transaction. In all ages of the world this eminently plausible fiction has lured the obtuse infant to financial ruin and disaster.

If at any time you find it necessary to correct your brother, do not correct him with mud—never on any account throw mud at him, because it will soil his clothes. It is better to scald him a little; for then you attain two desirable results—you secure his immediate attention to the lesson you are inculcating, and, at the same time, your hot water will have a tendency to remove impurities from his person—and possibly the skin also, in spots.

If your mother tells you to do a thing, it is wrong to reply that you won't. It is better and more becoming to intimate that you will do as she bids you, and then afterward act quietly in the matter according to the dictates of your better judgment.

You should ever bear in mind that it is to your kind parents that you are indebted for your food and your nice bed and your beautiful clothes, and for the privilege of staying home from school when you let on that you are sick. Therefore you ought to respect their little prejudices and humor their little whims and put up with their little foibles, until they get to crowding you too much.

Good little girls should always show marked deference for the aged. You ought never to "sass" old people—unless they "sass" you first.

1865

The Celebrated Jumping Frog of Calaveras County

IN compliance with the request of a friend of mine, who wrote me from the East, I called on good-natured, garrulous old Simon Wheeler, and inquired after my friend's friend, *Leonidas W.* Smiley, as requested to do, and I hereunto append the result. I have a lurking suspicion that *Leonidas W.* Smiley is a myth; that my friend never knew such a personage; and that he only conjectured that, if I asked old Wheeler about him, it would remind him of his infamous *Jim* Smiley, and he would go to work and bore me nearly to death with some infernal reminiscence of him as long and tedious as it should be useless to me. If that was the design, it certainly succeeded.

I found Simon Wheeler dozing comfortably by the bar-room stove of the old, dilapidated tavern in the ancient mining camp of Angel's, and I noticed that he was fat and bald-headed, and had an expression of winning gentleness and simplicity upon his tranquil countenance. He roused up and gave me good-day. I told him a friend of mine had commissioned me to make some inquiries about a cherished companion of his boyhood named *Leonidas W.* Smiley—*Rev. Leonidas W.* Smiley—a young minister of the Gospel, who he had heard was at one time a resident of Angel's Camp. I added that, if Mr. Wheeler could tell me any thing about this Rev. Leonidas W. Smiley, I would feel under many obligations to him.

Simon Wheeler backed me into a corner and blockaded me there with his chair, and then sat me down and reeled off the monotonous narrative which follows this paragraph. He never smiled, he never frowned, he never changed his voice from the gentle-flowing key to which he tuned the initial sentence, he never betrayed the slightest suspicion of enthusiasm; but all through the interminable narrative there ran a vein of impressive earnestness and sincerity, which showed me plainly that, so far from his imagining that there was any thing ridiculous or funny about his story, he regarded it as a really important matter, and admired its two heroes as men of transcendent genius in *finesse.* To me, the spectacle of a man drifting serenely along through such a queer yarn without ever smiling, was exquisitely absurd. As I said before, I asked him to tell me what he knew of Rev. Leonidas W. Smiley, and he replied as follows. I let him go on in his own way, and never interrupted him once:

There was a feller here once by the name of *Jim* Smiley, in the winter of '49—or may be it was the spring of '50—I don't recollect exactly, somehow, though what makes me think it was one or the other is because I remember the big flume wasn't finished when he first came to the camp; but any way, he was the curiosest man about always betting on any thing that turned up you ever see, if he could get any body to bet on the other side; and if he couldn't, he'd change sides.

Any way that suited the other man would suit him—any way just so's he got a bet, *he* was satisfied. But still he was lucky, uncommon lucky; he most always come out winner. He was always ready and laying for a chance; there couldn't be no solitry thing mentioned but that feller'd offer to bet on it, and take any side you please, as I was just telling you. If there was a horse-race, you'd find him flush, or you'd find him busted at the end of it; if there was a dog-fight, he'd bet on it; if there was a cat-fight, he'd bet on it; if there was a chicken-fight, he'd bet on it; why, if there was two birds setting on a fence, he would bet you which one would fly first; or if there was a camp-meeting, he would be there reg'lar, to bet on Parson Walker, which he judged to be the best exhorter about here, and so he was, too, and a good man. If he even seen a straddle-bug start to go anywheres, he would bet you how long it would take him to get wherever he was going to, and if you took him up, he would foller that straddle-bug to Mexico but what he would find out where he was bound for and how long he was on the road. Lots of the boys here has seen that Smiley, and can tell you about him. Why, it never made no difference to *him*—he would bet on *any* thing—the dangdest feller. Parson Walker's wife laid very sick once, for a good while, and it seemed as if they warn't going to save her; but one morning he come in, and Smiley asked how she was, and he said she was considerable better—thank the Lord for his inf'nit mercy—and coming on so smart that, with the blessing of Prov'dence, she'd get well yet; and Smiley, before he thought, says, "Well, I'll risk two-and-a-half that she don't, any way."

Thish-yer Smiley had a mare—the boys called her the fifteen-minute nag, but that was only in fun, you know, because, of course, she was faster than that—and he used to win money on that horse, for all she was so slow and always had the asthma, or the distemper, or the consumption, or something of that kind. They used to give her two or three hundred yards start, and then pass her under way; but always at the fag-end of the race she'd get excited and desperate-like, and come cavorting and straddling up, and scattering her legs around limber, sometimes in the air, and sometimes out to one side amongst the fences, and kicking up m-o-r-e dust, and raising m-o-r-e racket with her coughing and sneezing and blowing her nose—and always fetch up at the stand just about a neck ahead, as near as you could cipher it down.

And he had a little small bull pup, that to look at him you'd think he wan't worth a cent, but to set around and look ornery, and lay for a chance to steal something. But as soon as money was up on him, he was a different dog; his under-jaw'd begin to stick out like the fo'castle of a steamboat, and his teeth would uncover, and shine savage like the furnaces. And a dog might tackle him, and bully-rag him, and bite him, and throw him over his shoulder two or three times, and Andrew Jackson—which was the name of the pup—Andrew Jackson would never let on but what *he* was satisfied, and hadn't expected nothing else—and the bets being doubled and doubled on the other side all the time, till the money was all up; and then all of a sudden he would grab that other dog jest by the j'int of his hind leg and freeze to it—not chaw, you understand, but only jest grip and hang on till they throwed up the sponge, if it was a year. Smiley always come out winner on that pup, till he harnessed a dog once that didn't have no hind legs, because they'd been sawed off by a circular saw, and when the thing had gone along far enough, and the money was all up, and he come to make a snatch for his pet holt, he saw in a minute how he'd been imposed on, and how the other dog had him in the door, so to speak, and he 'peared surprised, and then he looked sorter discouraged-like, and didn't try no more to win the fight, and so he got shucked out bad. He give Smiley a look, as much as to say his heart was broke, and it was *his* fault, for putting up a dog that hadn't no hind legs for him to take holt of, which was his main dependence in a fight, and then he limped off a piece and laid down and died. It was a good pup, was that Andrew Jackson, and would have made a name for hisself if he'd lived, for the stuff was in him, and he had genius—I know it, because he hadn't had no opportunities to speak of, and it don't stand to reason that a dog could make such a fight as he could under them circumstances, if he hadn't no talent. It always makes me feel sorry when I think of that last fight of his'n, and the way it turned out.

Well, thish-yer Smiley had rat-tarriers, and chicken cocks, and tom-cats, and all them kind of things, till you couldn't rest, and you couldn't fetch nothing for him to bet on but he'd match you. He ketched a frog one day, and took him home, and said he cal'klated to edercate him; and so he never done nothing for three months but set in his back yard and learn that frog to jump. And you bet you he *did* learn him, too. He'd give him a little punch behind, and the next minute you'd see that frog whirling in the air like a doughnut—see him turn one summerset, or may be a couple, if he got a good start, and come down flat-footed and all right, like a cat. He got him up so in the matter of catching flies, and kept him in practice so constant, that he'd nail a fly every time as far as he could see him. Smiley said all a frog wanted was education, and he could do most any thing—and I believe him. Why, I've seen him set Dan'l Webster down here on this floor—Dan'l Webster was the name of the frog—and sing out, "Flies, Dan'l, flies!" and quicker'n you could wink, he'd spring straight up, and snake a fly off'n the counter there, and flop down on the floor again as solid as a gob of mud, and fall to scratching the side of his head with his hind foot as indifferent as if he hadn't no idea he'd been doin' any more'n any frog might do. You never see a frog so modest and straightfor'ard as he was, for all he was so gifted. And when it come to fair and square jumping on a dead level, he could get over more ground at one straddle than any animal of his breed you ever see. Jumping on a dead level was his strong suit, you understand; and when it come to that, Smiley would ante up money on him as long as he had a red. Smiley was monstrous proud of his frog, and well he might be, for fellers that had traveled and been everywheres, all said he laid over any frog that ever *they* see.

Well, Smiley kept the beast in a little lattice box, and he used to fetch him down town sometimes and lay for a bet. One day a feller—a stranger in the camp, he was—come across him with his box, and says:

"What might it be that you've got in the box?"

And Smiley says, sorter indifferent like, "It might be

a parrot, or it might be a canary, may be, but it an't—it's only just a frog."

And the feller took it, and looked at it careful, and turned it round this way and that, and says, "H'm—so 'tis. Well, what's *he* good for?"

"Well," Smiley says, easy and careless, "he's good enough for *one* thing, I should judge—he can outjump any frog in Calaveras county."

The feller took the box again, and took another long, particular look, and give it back to Smiley, and says, very deliberate, "Well, I don't see no p'ints about that frog that's any better'n any other frog."

"May be you don't," Smiley says. "May be you understand frogs, and may be you don't understand 'em; may be you've had experience, and may be you an't only a amature, as it were. Anyways, I've got *my* opinion, and I'll risk forty dollars that he can outjump any frog in Calaveras county."

And the feller studied a minute, and then says, kinder sad like, "Well, I'm only a stranger here, and I an't got no frog; but if I had a frog, I'd bet you."

And then Smiley says, "That's all right—that's all right—if you'll hold my box a minute, I'll go and get you a frog." And so the feller took the box, and put up his forty dollars along with Smiley's, and set down to wait.

So he set there a good while thinking and thinking to hisself, and then he got the frog out and prized his mouth open and took a teaspoon and filled him full of quail shot—filled him pretty near up to his chin—and set him on the floor. Smiley he went to the swamp and slopped around in the mud for a long time, and finally he ketched a frog, and fetched him in, and give him to this feller, and says:

"Now, if you're ready, set him alongside of Dan'l, with his fore-paws just even with Dan'l, and I'll give the word." Then he says, "One—two—three—jump!" and him and the feller touched up the frogs from behind, and the new frog hopped off, but Dan'l give a heave, and hysted up his shoulders—so—like a Frenchman, but it wan't no use—he couldn't budge; he was planted as solid as an anvil, and he couldn't no more stir than if he was anchored out. Smiley was a good deal surprised, and he was disgusted too, but he didn't have no idea what the matter was, of course.

The feller took the money and started away; and when he was going out at the door, he sorter jerked his thumb over his shoulder—this way—at Dan'l, and says again, very deliberate, "Well, *I* don't see no p'ints about that frog that's any better'n any other frog."

Smiley he stood scratching his head and looking down at Dan'l a long time, and at last he says, "I do wonder what in the nation that frog throw'd off for—I wonder if there an't something the matter with him—he 'pears to look mighty baggy, somehow." And he ketched Dan'l by the nap of the neck, and lifted him up and says, "Why, blame my cats, if he don't weigh five pound!" and turned him upside down, and he belched out a double handful of shot. And then he see how it was, and he was the maddest man—he set the frog down and took out after that feller, but he never ketched him. And—

[Here Simon Wheeler heard his name called from the front yard, and got up to see what was wanted.] And turning to me as he moved away, he said: "Just set where you are, stranger, and rest easy—I an't going to be gone a second."

But, by your leave, I did not think that a continuation of the history of the enterprising vagabond *Jim* Smiley would be likely to afford me much information concerning the Rev. *Leonidas W.* Smiley, and so I started away.

At the door I met the sociable Wheeler returning, and he buttonholed me and recommenced:

"Well, thish-yer Smiley had a yaller one-eyed cow that didn't have no tail, only jest a short stump like a bannanner, and—"

"Oh! hang Smiley and his afflicted cow!" I muttered, good-naturedly, and bidding the old gentleman good-day, I departed.

1865

The Story of the Bad Little Boy Who Didn't Come to Grief

ONCE there was a bad little boy, whose name was Jim—though, if you will notice, you will find that bad little boys are nearly always called James in your Sunday-school books. It was very strange, but still it was true, that this one was called Jim.

He didn't have any sick mother, either—a sick mother who was pious and had the consumption, and would be glad to lie down in the grave and be at rest, but for the strong love she bore her boy, and the anxiety she felt that the world would be harsh and cold towards him when she was gone. Most bad boys in the Sunday books are named James, and have sick mothers, who teach them to say, "Now I lay me down," etc., and sing them to sleep with sweet plaintive voices, and then kiss them goodnight, and kneel down by the bedside and weep. But it was different with this fellow. He was named Jim, and there wasn't any thing the matter with his mother—no consumption, or any thing of that kind. She was rather stout than otherwise, and she was not pious; moreover, she was not anxious on Jim's account. She said if he were to break his neck, it wouldn't be much loss. She always spanked Jim to sleep, and she never kissed him goodnight; on the contrary, she boxed his ears when she was ready to leave him.

Once this little bad boy stole the key of the pantry and slipped in there and helped himself to some jam, and filled up the vessel with tar, so that his mother would never know the difference; but all at once a terrible feeling didn't come over him, and something didn't seem to whisper to him, "Is it right to disobey my mother? Isn't it sinful to do this? Where do bad little boys go who gobble up their good kind mother's jam?" and then he didn't kneel down all alone and promise never to be wicked any more, and rise up with a light, happy heart, and go and tell his mother all about it, and beg her forgiveness, and be blessed by her with tears of pride and thankfulness in her eyes. No; that is the way with all other bad boys in the books; but it happened otherwise with this Jim, strangely enough. He ate that jam, and said it was bully, in his sinful, vulgar way; and he put in the tar, and said that was bully also, and laughed, and observed that "the old woman would get up and snort" when she found it out; and when she did find it out, he denied knowing any thing about it, and she whipped him severely, and he did the crying himself. Every thing about this boy was curious—every thing turned out differently with him from the way it does to the bad Jameses in the books.

Once he climbed up in Farmer Acorn's apple-tree to steal apples, and the limb didn't break, and he didn't fall and break his arm, and get torn by the farmer's great dog, and then languish on a sick bed for weeks, and repent and become good. Oh! no; he stole as many apples as he wanted, and came down all right; and he was all ready for the dog, too, and knocked him endways with a rock when he came to tear him. It was very strange—nothing like it ever happened in those mild little books with marbled backs, and with pictures in them of men with swallow-tailed coats, and bell-crowned hats, and pantaloons that are short in the legs, and women with the waists of their dresses under their arms and no hoops on. Nothing like it in any of the Sunday-school books.

Once he stole the teacher's penknife, and when he was afraid it would be found out, and he would get whipped, he slipped it into George Wilson's cap—poor Widow Wilson's son, the moral boy, the good little boy of the village, who always obeyed his mother, and never told an untruth, and was fond of his lessons and infatuated with Sunday-school. And when the knife dropped from the cap, and poor George hung his head and blushed, as if in conscious guilt, and the grieved teacher charged the theft upon him, and was just in the very act of bringing the switch down upon his trembling shoulders, a white-haired improbable justice of the peace did not suddenly appear in their midst and strike an attitude and say, "spare this noble boy—there stands the cowering culprit! I was passing the school-door at recess, and, unseen myself, I saw the theft committed!" And then Jim didn't get whaled, and the venerable justice didn't read the tearful school a homily, and take George by the hand and say such a boy deserved to be exalted, and then tell him to come and make his home with him, and sweep out the office, and make fires, and run errands, and chop wood, and study law, and help his wife to do household labors, and have all the balance of the time to play, and get forty cents a month, and be happy. No; it would have happened that way in the books, but it didn't happen that way to Jim. No meddling old clam of a justice dropped in to make trouble, and so the model boy George got threshed, and Jim was glad of it; because, you know, Jim hated moral boys. Jim said he was "down on them milksops." Such was the coarse language of this bad, neglected boy.

But the strangest things that ever happened to Jim was the time he went boating on Sunday and didn't get drowned, and that other time that he got caught out in the storm when he was fishing on Sunday, and didn't get struck by lightning. Why, you might look, and look, and look through the Sunday-school books, from now till next Christmas, and you would never come across any thing like this. Oh! no; you would find that all the bad boys who go boating on Sunday invariably get drowned; and all the bad boys who get caught out in storms, when they are fishing on Sunday, infallibly get struck by lightning. Boats with bad boys in them always upset on Sunday, and it always storms when bad boys go fishing on the Sabbath. How this Jim ever escaped is a mystery to me.

This Jim bore a charmed life—that must have been the way of it. Nothing could hurt him. He even gave the elephant in the menagerie a plug of tobacco, and the elephant didn't knock the top of his head off with his trunk. He browsed around the cupboard after essence of peppermint, and didn't make a mistake and drink aqua fortis. He stole his father's gun and went hunting on the Sabbath, and didn't shoot three or four of his fingers off. He struck his little sister on the temple with his fist when he was angry, and she didn't linger in pain through long summer days, and die with sweet words of forgiveness upon her lips that redoubled the anguish of his breaking heart. No; she got over it. He ran off and went to sea at last, and didn't come back and find himself sad and alone in the world, his loved ones sleeping in the quiet churchyard, and the vine-embowered home of his boyhood tumbled down and gone to decay. Ah! no; he came home drunk as a piper, and got into the station-house the first thing.

And he grew up, and married, and raised a large family, and brained them all with an ax one night, and got wealthy by all manner of cheating and rascality, and now he is the infernalest wickedest scoundrel in his native village, and is universally respected, and belongs to the Legislature.

So you see there never was a bad James in the Sunday-school books that had such a streak of luck as this sinful Jim with the charmed life.

1865

Answers to Correspondents

"MORAL STATISTICIAN."—I don't want any of your statistics. I took your whole batch and lit my pipe with it. I hate your kind of people. You are always ciphering out how much a man's health is injured, and how much his intellect is impaired, and how many pitiful dollars and cents he wastes in the course of ninety-two years' indulgence in the fatal practice of smoking; and in the equally fatal practice of drinking coffee; and in playing billiards occasionally; and in taking a glass of wine at dinner, etc., etc., etc. And you are always figuring out how many women have been burned to death because of the dangerous fashion of wearing expansive hoops, etc., etc., etc. You never see more than one side of the question. You are blind to the fact that most old men in America smoke and drink coffee, although, according to your theory, they ought to have died young; and that hearty old Englishmen drink wine and survive it, and portly old Dutchmen both drink and smoke freely, and yet grow older and fatter all the time. And you never try to find out how much solid comfort, relaxation, and enjoyment a man derives from smoking in the course of a lifetime, (which is worth ten times the money he would save by letting it alone,) nor the appalling aggregate of happiness lost in a lifetime by your kind of people from *not* smoking. Of course you can save money by denying yourself all these little vicious enjoyments for fifty years; but then what can you do with it? What use can you put it to? Money can't save your infinitesimal soul. All the use that money can be put to is to purchase comfort and enjoyment in this life; therefore, as you are an enemy to comfort and enjoyment, where is the use in accumulating cash? It won't do for you to say that you can use it to better purpose in furnishing a good table, and in charities, and in supporting tract societies, because you know yourself that you people who have no petty vices are never known to give away a cent, and that you stint yourselves so in the matter of food that you are always feeble and hungry. And you never dare to laugh in the daytime for fear some poor wretch, seeing you in a good humor, will try to borrow a dollar of you; and in church you are always down on your knees, with your eyes buried in the cushion, when the contribution-box comes around; and you never give the revenue officers a true statement of your income. Now you know all these things yourself, don't you? Very well, then, what is the use of your stringing out your miserable lives to a lean and withered old age? What is the use of your saving money that is so utterly worthless to you? In a word, why don't you go off somewhere and die, and not be always trying to seduce people into becoming as "ornery" and unlovable as you are yourselves, by your ceaseless and villainous "moral statistics"? Now, I don't approve of dissipation, and I don't indulge in it, either; but I haven't a particle of confidence in a man who has no redeeming petty vices whatever, and so I don't want to hear from you any more. I think you are the very same man who read me a long lecture, last week, about the degrading vice of smoking cigars, and then came back, in my absence, with your vile, reprehensible fire-proof gloves on, and carried off my beautiful parlor-stove.

———

"SIMON WHEELER," *Sonora*.—The following simple and touching remarks and accompanying poem have just come to hand from the rich gold-mining region of Sonora :

To Mr. Mark Twain: The within parson, which I have sot to poettry under the name and style of "He Done His Level Best," was one among the whitest men I ever see, and it an't every man that knowed him that can find it in his heart to say he's glad the poor cuss is busted and gone home to the states. He was here in an early day, and he was the handyest man about takin' holt of any thing that come along you most ever see, I judge. He was a cheerful, stirrin' cretur', always doin' something, and no man can say he ever see him do any thing by halvers. Preachin' was his nateral gait, but he warn't a man to lay back and twidle his thums because there didn't happen to he nothin' doin' in his own espeshial line—no, sir, he was a man who would meander forth and stir up something for his-self. His last acts was to go his pile on "kings-*and*," (calklatin' to fill, but which he didn't fill,) when there was a "flush" out agin him, and naterally, you see, he went under. And so he was cleaned out, as you may say, and he struck the home-trail, cheerful but flat broke. I knewed this talonted man in Arkansaw, and if you would print this humbly tribute to his gorgis abillities, you would greatly obleege his onhappy friend.

HE DONE HIS LEVEL BEST.

Was he a mining on the flat—
He done it with a zest;
Was he a leading of the choir—
He done his level best.

If he'd a reg'lar task to do,
He never took no rest;
Or if 'twas off-and-on—the same—
He done his level best.

If he was preachin' on his beat,
He'd tramp from east to west,
And north to south—in cold and heat
He done his level best.

He'd yank a sinner outen (Hades),*
And land him with the blest;
Then snatch a prayer 'n waltz in again,
And do his level best.

He'd cuss and sing and howl and pray,
And dance and drink and jest,
And lie and steal—all one to him—
He done his level best.

Whate'er this man was sot to do,
He done it with a zest;
No matter what his contract was,
HE'D DO HIS LEVEL BEST.

Verily, this man *was* gifted with "gorgis abillities," and it is a happiness to me to embalm the memory of their lustre in these columns. If it were not that the poet crop is unusually large and rank in California this year, I would encourage you to continue writing, Simon; but as it is, perhaps it might be too risky in you to enter against so much opposition.

* Here I have taken a slight liberty with the original MS. "Hades" does not make such good metre as the other word of one syllable, but it sounds better.

"INQUIRER" wishes to know which is the best brand of smoking tobacco, and how it is manufactured. The most popular—mind, I do not feel at liberty to give an opinion as to the best, and so I simply say the most popular—smoking tobacco is the miraculous conglomerate they call "Killikinick." It is composed of equal parts of tobacco stems, chopped straw, "old soldiers," fine shavings, oak leaves, dog-fennel, corn-shucks, sunflower petals, outside leaves of the cabbage plant, and any refuse of any description whatever that costs nothing and will burn. After the ingredients are thoroughly mixed together, they are run through a chopping-machine and soaked in a spittoon. The mass is then sprinkled with fragrant Scotch snuff, packed into various seductive shapes, labeled "Genuine Killikinick, from the old original manufactory at Richmond," and sold to consumers at a dollar a pound. The choicest brands contain a double portion of "old soldiers," and sell at a dollar and a half. "Genuine Turkish" tobacco contains a treble quantity of "old soldiers," and is worth two or three dollars, according to the amount of service the said "old soldiers" have previously seen. N. B.—This article is preferred by the Sultan of Turkey; his picture and autograph are on the label. Take a handful of "Killikinick," crush it as fine as you can, and examine it closely, and you will find that you can make as good an analysis of it as I have done; you must not expect to discover any particles of genuine tobacco by this rough method, however—to do that, it will be necessary to take your specimen to the mint and subject it to a fire-assay. A good article of cheap tobacco is now made of chopped pine-straw and

Spanish moss; it contains one "old soldier" to the ton, and is called "Fine Old German Tobacco."

"PROFESSIONAL BEGGAR."—No; you are not obliged to take greenbacks at par.

* "Melton Mowbray," *Dutch Flat*.—This correspondent sends a lot of doggerel, and says it has been regarded as very good in Dutch Flat. I give a specimen verse:

"The Assyrian came down, like a wolf on the fold,
And his cohorts were gleaming in purple and gold;
And the sheen of his spears shone like stars on the sea,
When the blue wave rolls nightly on deep Galilee."

There, that will do. That may be very good Dutch Flat poetry, but it won't do in the metropolis. It is too smooth and blubbery; it reads like buttermilk gurgling from a jug. What the people ought to have is something spirited—something like "Johnny Comes Marching Home." However, keep on practicing, and you may succeed yet. There is genius in you, but too much blubber.

"AMATEUR SERENADER."—Yes, I will give you some advice, and do it with a good deal of pleasure. I live in a neighborhood which is well stocked with young ladies,

* This piece of pleasantry, published in a San Francisco paper, was mistaken by the country journals for seriousness, and many and loud were their denunciations of the ignorance of author and editor, in not knowing that the lines in question were "written by Byron."

and consequently I am excruciatingly sensitive upon the subject of serenading. Sometimes I suffer. In the first place, always tune your instruments before you get within three hundred yards of your destination. This will enable you to take your adored unawares, and create a pleasant surprise by launching out at once upon your music. It astonishes the dogs and cats out of their presence of mind, too, so that, if you hurry, you can get through before they have a chance to recover and interrupt you; besides, there is nothing captivating in the sounds produced in tuning a lot of melancholy guitars and fiddles, and neither does a group of able-bodied, sentimental young men so engaged look at all dignified. Secondly, clear your throats and do all the coughing you have got to do before you arrive at the seat of war. I have known a young lady to be ruthlessly startled out of her slumbers by such a sudden and direful blowing of noses and "h'm-h'm-ing" and coughing, that she imagined the house was beleaguered by victims of consumption from the neighboring hospital. Do you suppose the music was able to make her happy after that? Thirdly, don't stand right under the porch and howl, but get out in the middle of the street, or better still, on the other side of it. Distance lends enchantment to the sound. If you have previously transmitted a hint to the lady that she is going to be serenaded, she will understand whom the music is for; besides, if you occupy a neutral position in the middle of the street, may be all the neighbors round will take stock in your serenade, and invite you to take wine with them. Fourthly, don't sing a whole opera through; enough of a thing's enough. Fifthly, don't sing "Lily Dale." The profound satisfaction that most of us derive from the reflection that the girl treated of in that song is dead, is constantly marred by the resurrection of the lugubrious ditty itself by your kind of people. Sixthly, don't let your screaming tenor soar an octave above all the balance of the chorus, and remain there setting every body's teeth on edge for four blocks around; and, above all, don't let him sing a solo; probably there is nothing in the world so suggestive of serene contentment and perfect bliss as the spectacle of a calf chewing a dish-rag; but the nearest approach to it is your reedy tenor, standing apart, in sickly attitude, with head thrown back and eyes uplifted to the moon, piping his distressing solo. Now do not pass lightly over this matter, friend, but ponder it with that seriousness which its importance entitles it to. Seventhly, after you have run all the chickens and dogs and cats in the vicinity distracted, and roused them into a frenzy of crowing, and cackling, and yawling, and caterwauling, put up your dreadful instruments and go home. Eighthly, as soon as you start, gag your tenor—otherwise he will be letting off a screech every now and then, to let the people know he is around. Your amateur tenor is notoriously the most self-conceited of all God's creatures. Tenthly, don't go serenading at all; it is a wicked, unhappy, and seditious practice, and a calamity to all souls that are weary and desire to slumber and would be at rest. Eleventhly and lastly, the father of the young lady in the next block says that if you come prowling around his neighborhood again, with your infamous scraping and tooting and yelling, he will sally forth and deliver you into the hands of the police. As far as I am concerned myself, I would like to have you come, and come often; but as long as the old man is so prejudiced, perhaps you had better serenade mostly in Oakland, or San José, or around there somewhere.

"ST. CLAIR HIGGINS," *Los Angles*.—" My life is a failure; I have adored, wildly, madly, and she whom I love has turned coldly from me and shed her affections upon another. What would you advise me to do?"

You should shed your affections on another, also—or on several, if there are enough to go round. Also, do every thing you can to make your former flame unhappy. There is an absurd idea disseminated in novels, that the happier a girl is with another man, the happier it makes the old lover she has blighted. Don't allow yourself to believe any such nonsense as that. The more cause that girl finds to regret that she did not marry you, the more comfortable you will feel over it. It isn't poetical, but it is mighty sound doctrine.

"ARITHMETICUS," *Virginia, Nevada*.—"If it would take a cannon ball 3 1/3 seconds to travel four miles, and 3 3/8 seconds to travel the next four, and 3 5/8 seconds to travel the next four, and if its rate of progress continued to diminish in the same ratio, how long would it take it to go fifteen hundred millions of miles?"

I don't know.

"AMBITIOUS LEARNER," *Oakland*.—Yes, you are right—America was not discovered by Alexander Selkirk.

"DISCARDED LOVER."—" I loved, and still love, the beautiful Edwitha Howard, and intended to marry her. Yet, during my temporary absence at Benicia, last week, alas! she married Jones. Is my happiness to be thus blasted for life? Have I no redress?"

Of course you have. All the law, written and unwritten, is on your side. The *intention* and not the *act* constitutes crime—in other words, constitutes the *deed*. If you call your bosom friend a fool, and *intend* it for an insult, it *is* an insult; but if you do it playfully, and meaning no insult, it is *not* an insult. If you discharge a pistol *accidentally*, and kill a man, you can go free, for you have done no murder; but if you try to kill a man, and manifestly *intend* to kill him, but fall utterly to do it, the law still holds that the *intention* constituted the crime, and you are guilty of murder. Ergo, if you had married Edwitha *accidentally*, and without really *intending* to do it, you would not actually be married to her at all, because the *act* of marriage could not be complete without the *intention*. And ergo, in the strict spirit of the law, since you deliberately *intended* to marry Edwitha, and didn't do it, you are married to her all the same—because, as I said before, the *intention* constitutes the crime. It is as clear as day that Edwitha is your wife, and your redress lies in taking a club and mutilating Jones with it as much as you can. Any man has a right to protect his own wife from the advances of other men. But you have another alternative—you were married to Edwitha *first*, because of your deliberate intention, and now you can prosecute her for bigamy, in subsequently marrying Jones. But there is another phase in this complicated case: You *intended* to marry Edwitha, and consequently, according to law, she is your wife—there is no getting around that; but she didn't marry you, and if she *never intended* to marry you, *you are not her husband*, of course. Ergo, in marrying Jones, she was guilty of bigamy, because she was the wife of another man at the time; which is all very well as far as it goes—but then, don't you see, she had no other *husband* when she married Jones, and consequently she was *not* guilty of bigamy. Now, according to this view of the case, Jones married a *spinster*, who was a *widow* at the same time and another man's *wife* at the same time, and yet who had no *husband* and *never had one*, and never had any *intention* of getting married, and therefore, of course, *never had* been married; and by the same reasoning you are a *bachelor*, because you have never been any one's *husband*; and a *married man*, because you have a wife living; and to all intents and purposes a *widower*, because you have been deprived of that wife; and a consummate *ass* for going off to Benicia in the first place, while things were so mixed. And by this time I have got myself so tangled up in the intricacies of this extraordinary case that I shall have to give up any further attempt to advise you—I might get confused and fail to make myself understood. I think I could take up the argument where I left off, and by following it closely awhile, perhaps I could prove to your satisfaction, either that you never existed at all, or that you are dead now, and consequently don't need the faithless Edwitha—I think I could do that, if it would afford you any comfort.

"PERSECUTED UNFORTUNATE."—You say you owe six months' board, and you have no money to pay it with, and your landlord keeps harassing you about it, and you have made all the excuses and explanations possible, and now you are at a loss what to say to him in future. Well, it is a delicate matter to offer advice in a case like this, but your distress impels me to make a suggestion, at least, since I can not venture to do more. When he next importunes you, how would it do to take him impressively by the hand and ask, with simulated emotion, "*Monsieur Jean, votre chien, comme se porteil?*" Doubtless that is very bad French, but you will find that it will answer just as well as the unadulterated article.

"ARTHUR AUGUSTUS."—No, you are wrong; that is the proper way to throw a brickbat or a tomahawk; but it doesn't answer so well for a bouquet; you will hurt somebody if you keep it up. Turn your nosegay upside down, take it by the stems, and toss it with an upward sweep. Did you ever pitch quoits? that is the idea. The practice of recklessly heaving immense solid bouquets, of the general size and weight of prize cabbages, from the dizzy altitude of the galleries, is dangerous and very reprehensible. Now, night before last, at the Academy of Music, just after Signorina Sconcia had finished that exquisite melody, "The Last Rose of Summer," one of these floral pile-drivers came cleaving down through the atmosphere of applause, and if she hadn't deployed suddenly to the right, it would have driven her into the floor like a shingle-nail. Of course that bouquet was well meant; but how would you have liked to have been the target? A sincere compliment is always grateful to a lady, so long as you don't try to knock her down with it.

"YOUNG MOTHER."—And so you think a baby is a thing of beauty and a joy forever? Well, the idea is pleasing, but not original; every cow thinks the same of its own calf. Perhaps the cow may not think it so elegantly, but still she thinks it, nevertheless. I honor the cow for it. We all honor this touching maternal instinct wherever we find it, be it in the home of luxury or in the humble cow-shed. But really, madam, when I come to examine the matter in all its bearings, I find that the correctness of your assertion does not manifest itself in all cases. A sore-faced baby, with a neglected nose, can not be conscientiously regarded as a thing of beauty; and inasmuch as babyhood spans but three short years, no baby is competent to be a joy "forever." It pains me thus to demolish two thirds of your pretty sentiment in a single sentence; but the position I hold in this chair requires that I shall not permit you to deceive and mislead the public with your plausible figures of speech. I know a female baby, aged eighteen months, in this city, which can not hold out as a "joy" twenty-four hours on a stretch, let alone "forever." And it possesses some of the most remarkable eccentricities of character and appetite that have ever fallen under my notice. I will set down here a statement of this infant's operations, (conceived, planned, and carried out by itself, and without suggestion or assistance from its mother or any one else,) during a single day; and what I shall say can be substantiated by the sworn testimony of witnesses.

It commenced by eating one dozen large blue-mass pills, box and all; then it fell down a flight of stairs, and arose with a bruised and purple knot on its forehead, after which it proceeded in quest of further refreshment and amusement. It found a glass trinket ornamented with brasswork—mashed up and ate the glass, and then swallowed the brass. Then it drank about twenty drops of laudanum, and more than a dozen table-spoonfuls of strong spirits of camphor. The reason why it took no more laudanum was because there was no more to take. After this it lay down on its back, and shoved five or six inches of a silver-headed whalebone cane down its throat; got it fast there, and it was all its mother could do to pull the cane out again, without pulling out some of the child with it. Then, being hungry for glass again, it broke up several wine glasses, and fell to eating and swallowing the fragments, not minding a cut or two. Then it ate a quantity of butter, pepper, salt, and California matches, actually taking a spoonful of butter, a spoonful of salt, a spoonful of pepper, and three or four lucifer matches at each mouthful. (I will remark here that this thing of beauty likes painted German lucifers, and eats all she can get of them; but she infinitely prefers California matches, which I regard as a compliment to our home manufactures of more than ordinary value, coming, as it does, from one who is too young to flatter.) Then she washed her head with soap and water, and afterward ate what soap was left, and drank as much of the suds as she had room for; after which she sallied forth and took the cow familiarly by the tail, and got kicked heels over head. At odd times during the day, when this joy forever happened to have nothing particular on hand, she put in the time by climbing up on places, and falling down off them, uniformly damaging herself in the operation.

As young as she is, she speaks many words tolerably distinctly; and being plain-spoken in other respects, blunt and to the point, she opens conversation with all strangers, male or female, with the same formula, "How do, Jim ?" Not being familiar with the ways of children, it is possible that I have been magnifying into matter of surprise things which may not strike any one who is familiar with infancy as being at all astonishing. However, I can not believe that such is the case, and so I repeat that my report of this baby's performances is strictly true; and if any one doubts it, I can produce the child. I will further engage that she will devour any thing that is given her, (reserving to myself only the right to exclude anvils,) and fall down from any place to which she may be elevated, (merely stipulating that her preference for alighting on her head shall be respected, and, therefore, that the elevation chosen shall be high enough to enable her to accomplish this to her satisfaction.) But I find I have wandered from my subject; so, without further argument, I will reiterate my conviction that not *all* babies are things of beauty and joys forever.

"ARITHEMETICUS," *Virginia, Nevada.*—"I am an enthusiastic student of mathematics, and it is so vexatious to me to find my progress constantly impeded by these mysterious arithmetical technicalities. Now do tell me what the difference is between geometry and conchology ?"

Here *you* come again, with your diabolical arithmetical conundrums, when I am suffering death with a cold in the head. If you could have seen the expression of ineffable scorn that darkened my countenance a moment ago and was instantly split from the center in every direction like a fractured looking-glass by my last sneeze, you never would have written that disgraceful question. Conchology is a science which has nothing to do with mathematics; it relates only to shells. At the same time, however, a man who opens oysters for a hotel, or shells a fortified town, or sucks eggs, is not, strictly speaking, a conchologist—a fine stroke of sarcasm, that, but it will be lost on such an intellectual clam as you. Now compare conchology and geometry together, and you will see what the difference is, and your question will be answered. But don't torture me with any more of your ghastly arithmetical horrors (for I do detest figures any how) until you know I am rid of my cold. I feel the bitterest animosity toward you at this moment—bothering me in this way, when I can do nothing but sneeze and swear and snort pocket-handkerchiefs to atoms. If I had you in range of my nose, now, I would blow your brains out.

"SOCRATES MURPHY."—You speak of having given offense to a gentleman at the opera by *unconsciously* humming an air which the tenor was singing at the time. Now, part of that is a deliberate falsehood. You were not doing it "unconsciously;" no man does such a mean, vulgar, egotistical thing as that unconsciously. You were doing it to "show off;" you wanted the people around you to know you had been to operas before, and to think you were not such an ignorant, self-conceited, supercilious ass as you looked. I can tell you Arizona opera-sharps, any time; you prowl around beer cellars and listen to some howling-dervish of a Dutchman exterminating an Italian air, and then you come into the Academy and prop yourself up against the wall with the stuffy aspect and the imbecile leer of a clothing store dummy, and go to droning along about half an octave below the tenor, and disgusting every body in your neighborhood with your beery strains. [N. B.—If this rough-shod eloquence of mine touches you on a raw spot occasionally, recollect that I am talking for your good, Murphy, and that I am simplifying my language so as to bring it clearly within the margin of your comprehension; it might be gratifying to you to be addressed as if you were an Oxford graduate, but then you wouldn't understand it, you know.] You have got another abominable habit, my sage-brush amateur. When one of those Italian footmen in British uniform comes in and sings, "O tol de rol!—O Signo-o-o-ra!—loango—congo—Venezue-e-e-la! whack fol de rol!" (which means, "O noble madame! here's one of them dukes from the palace, out here, come to borrow a dollar and a half,") you always stand with expanded eyes and mouth, and one pile-driver uplifted, and your sprawling hands held apart in front of your face, like a couple of canvas-covered hams, and when he gets almost through, how you do uncork your pent-up enthusiasm, and applaud with hoof and palm! You have it pretty much to yourself, and then you look sheepish when you find every body staring at you. But how very idiotic you do look when something really fine is sung—you generally keep quiet, then. Never mind, though, Murphy, entire audiences do things at the opera that they have no business to do; for instance, they never let one of those thousand-dollar singers finish—they always break in with their ill-timed applause, just as he or she, as the case may be, is preparing to throw all his or her concentrated sweetness into the final strain, and so all that sweetness is lost. Write me again, Murphy, I shall always be happy to hear from you.

1865

Concerning Chambermaids

AGAINST all chambermaids, of whatsoever age or nationality, I launch the curse of bachelordom! Because:

They always put the pillows at the opposite end of the bed from the gas-burner, so that while you read and smoke before sleeping, (as is the ancient and honored custom of bachelors,) you have to hold your book aloft, in an uncomfortable position, to keep the light from dazzling your eyes.

When they find the pillows removed to the other end of the bed in the morning, they receive not the suggestion in a friendly spirit; but, glorying in their absolute sovereignty, and unpitying your helplessness, they make the bed just as it was originally, and gloat in secret over the pang their tyranny will cause you.

Always after that, when they find you have transposed the pillows, they undo your work, and thus defy and seek to embitter the life that God has given you.

If they can not get the light in an inconvenient position any other way, they move to bed.

If you pull your trunk out six inches from the wall, so that the lid will stay up when you open it, they always shove that trunk back again. They do it on purpose.

If you want the spittoon in a certain spot, where it will be handy, they don't, and so they move it.

They always put your other boots into inaccessible places. They chiefly enjoy depositing them as far under the bed as the wall will permit. It is because this compels you to get down in an undignified attitude and make wild sweeps for them in the dark with the boot-jack, and swear.

They always put the match-box in some other place. They hunt up a new place for it every day, and put up a bottle, or other perishable glass thing, where the box stood before. This is to cause you to break that glass thing, groping in the dark, and get yourself into trouble.

They are forever and ever moving the furniture. When you come in, in the night, you can calculate on finding the bureau where the wardrobe was in the morning. And when you go out in the morning, if you leave the slop-bucket by the door and rocking-chair by the window, when you come in at midnight, or thereabouts, you will fall over that rocking-chair, and you will proceed toward the window and sit down in that slop-tub. This will disgust you. They like that.

No matter where you put any thing, they are not going to let it stay there. They will take it and move it the first chance they get. It is their nature. And, besides, it gives them pleasure to be mean and contrary this way. They would die if they couldn't be villains.

They always save up all the old scraps of printed rubbish you throw on the floor, and stack them up carefully on the table, and start the fire with your valuable manuscripts. If there is any one particular old scrap that you are more down on than any other, and which you are gradually wearing your life out trying to get rid of, you may take all the pains you possibly can in that direction, but it won't be of any use, because they will always fetch that old scrap back and put it in the same old place again every time. It does them good.

And they use up more hair-oil than any six men. If charged with purloining the same, they lie about it. What do they care about a hereafter? Absolutely nothing.

If you leave your key in the door for convenience sake, they will carry it down to the office and give it to the clerk. They do this under the vile pretense of trying to protect your property from thieves; but actually they do it because they want to make you tramp back downstairs after it when you come home tired, or put you to the trouble of sending a waiter for it, which waiter will expect you to pay him something. In which case I suppose the degraded creatures divide.

They keep always trying to make your bed before you get up, thus destroying your rest and inflicting agony upon you; but after you get up, they don't come any more till next day.

They do all the mean things they can think of, and they do them just out of pure cussedness, and nothing else.

Chambermaids are dead to every human instinct.

I have cursed them in behalf of outraged bachelordom. They deserve it. If I can get a bill through the Legislature abolishing chambermaids, I mean to do it.

1866

An Inquiry About Insurances

COMING down from Sacramento the other night, I found on a center-table in the saloon of the steamboat, a pamphlet advertisement of an Accident Insurance Company. It interested me a good deal, with its General Accidents, and its Hazardous Tables, and Extra-Hazardous furniture of the same description, and I would like to know something more about it. It is a new thing to me. I want to invest if I come to like it. I want to ask merely a few questions of the man who carries on this Accident shop. For I am an orphan.

He publishes this list as accidents he is willing to insure people against.

General accidents include the Traveling Risk, and also all forms of Dislocations, Broken Bones, Ruptures, Tendons, Sprains, Concussions, Crushings, Bruising, Cuts, Stabs, Gun-shot Wounds, Poisoned Wounds, Burns and Scalds, Freezing, Bites, Unprovoked Assaults by Burglars, Robbers, or Murderers, the action of Lightning or Sunstroke, the effects of Explosions, Chemicals, Floods, and Earthquakes, Suffocation by Drowning or Choking—where such accidental injury totally disables the person insured from following his usual avocation, or causes death within three months from the time of the happening of the injury.

I want to address this party as follows:

Now, Smith—I suppose likely your name is Smith—you don't know me and I don't know you, but I am willing to be friendly. I am acquainted with a good many of your family—I know John as well as I know any man—and I think we can come to an understanding about your little game without any hard feelings. For instance:

Do you allow the same money on a dog-bite that you do on an earthquake? Do you take special risks for specific accidents?—that is to say, could I, by getting a policy for dog-bites alone, get it cheaper than if I took a chance in your whole lottery? And if so, and supposing I got insured against earthquakes, would you charge any more for San Francisco earthquakes than for those that prevail in places that are better anchored down? And if I had a policy on earthquakes alone, I couldn't collect on a dog-bite, may be, could I?

If a man had such a policy, and an earthquake shook him up and loosened his joints a good deal, but not enough to incapacitate him from engaging in pursuits which did not require him to be tight, wouldn't you pay him some of his pension? I notice you do not mention Biles. How about Biles? Why do you discriminate between Provoked and Unprovoked Assaults by Burglars? If a burglar entered my house at dead of night, and I, in the excitement natural to such an occasion, should forget myself and say something that provoked him, and he should cripple me, wouldn't I get any thing? But if I provoked him by pure accident, I would have you there, I judge; because you would have to pay for the Accident part of it any how, seeing that insuring against accidents is just your strong suit, you know. Now, that item about protecting a man against freezing is good. It will procure you all the custom you want in this country. Because, you understand, the people hereabouts have suffered a good deal from just such climatic drawbacks as that. Why, three years ago, if a man—being a small fish in the matter of money—went over to Washoe, and bought into a good silver mine, they would let that man go on and pay assessments till his purse got down to about thirty-two Fahrenheit, and then the big fish would close in on him and freeze him out. And from that day forth you might consider that man in the light of a bankrupt community; and you would have him down to a spot, too. But if you are ready to insure against that sort of thing, and can stand it, you can give Washoe a fair start. You might send me an agency. Business? Why, Smith, I could get you more business than you could attend to. With such an understanding as that, the boys would all take a chance.

You don't appear to make any particular mention of taking risks on blighted affections. But if you should conclude to do a little business in that line, you might put me down for six or seven chances. I wouldn't mind expense—you might enter it on the extra hazardous. I suppose I would get ahead of you in the long run any how, likely. I have been blighted a good deal in my time.

But now as to those "Effects of Lightning." Suppose the lightning were to strike out at one of your men and miss him, and fetch another party—could that other party come on you for damages? Or could the relatives of the party thus suddenly snaked out of the bright world in the bloom of his youth come on you in case he was crowded for time? As of course he would be, you know, under such circumstances.

You say you have "issued over sixty thousand policies, forty-five of which have proved fatal and been paid for." Now, do you know, Smith, that that looks just a little shaky to me, in a measure? You appear to have it pretty much all your own way, you see. It is all very well for the lucky forty-five that have died "and been paid for," but how about the other fifty-nine thousand nine hundred and fifty-five? You have got their money, haven't you? But somehow the lightning don't seem to strike them and they don't get any chance at you. Won't their families get fatigued waiting for their dividends? Don't your customers drop off rather slow, so to speak?

You will ruin yourself publishing such damaging statements as that, Smith. I tell you as a friend. If you had said that the fifty-nine thousand nine hundred and fifty-five died, and that forty-five lived, you would have issued about four tons of policies the next week. But people are not going to get insured, when you take so much pains to prove that there is such precious little use in it. Good-by Smith!

1866

Cannibalism in the Cars

I VISITED St. Louis lately, and on my way west, after changing cars at Terre Haute, Indiana, a mild, benevolent-looking gentleman of about forty-five, or may be fifty, came in at one of the way-stations and sat down beside me. We talked together pleasantly on various subjects for an hour, perhaps, and I found him exceedingly intelligent and entertaining. When he learned that I was from Washington, he immediately began to ask questions about various public men, and about Congressional affairs; and I saw very shortly that I was conversing with a man who was perfectly familiar with the ins and outs of political life at the Capital, even to the ways and manners, and customs of procedure of Senators and Representatives in the Chambers of the National Legislature. Presently two men halted near us for a single moment, and one said to the other:

"Harris, if you'll do that for me, I'll never forget you, my boy."

My new comrade's eyes lighted pleasantly. The words had touched upon a happy memory, I thought. Then his face settled into thoughtfulness—almost into gloom. He turned to me and said, "Let me tell you a story; let me give you a secret chapter of my life—a chapter that has never been referred to by me since its events transpired. Listen patiently, and promise that you will not interrupt me."

I said I would not, and he related the following strange adventure, speaking sometimes with animation, sometimes with melancholy, but always with feeling and earnestness.

THE STRANGER'S NARRATIVE.

"On the 19th of December, 1853, I started from St. Louis on the evening train bound for Chicago. There were only twenty-four passengers, all told. There were no ladies and no children. We were in excellent spirits, and pleasant acquaintanceships were soon formed. The journey bade fair to be a happy one; and no individual in the party, I think, had even the vaguest presentiment of the horrors we were soon to undergo.

"At 11 P. M. it began to snow hard. Shortly after leaving the small village of Welden, we entered upon that tremendous prairie solitude that stretches its leagues on leagues of houseless dreariness far away towards the Jubilee Settlements. The winds, unobstructed by trees or hills, or even vagrant rocks, whistled fiercely across the level desert, driving the falling snow before it like spray from the crested waves of a stormy sea. The snow was deepening fast; and we knew, by the diminished speed of the train, that the engine was ploughing through it with steadily increasing difficulty. Indeed, it almost came to a dead halt sometimes, in the midst of great drifts that piled themselves like colossal graves across the track. Conversation began to flag. Cheerfulness gave place to grave concern. The possibility of being imprisoned in the snow, on the bleak prairie, fifty miles from any house, presented itself to every mind, and extended its depressing influence over every spirit.

"At two o'clock in the morning I was aroused out of an uneasy slumber by the ceasing of all motion about me. The appalling truth flashed upon me instantly—we were captives in a snow-drift! 'All hands to the rescue!' Every man sprang to obey. Out into the wild night, the pitchy darkness, the billowy snow, the driving storm, every soul leaped, with the consciousness that a moment lost now might bring destruction to us all. Shovels, hands, boards—anything, everything that could displace snow, was brought into instant requisition. It was a weird picture, that small company of frantic men fighting the banking snows, half in the blackest shadow and half in the angry light of the locomotive's reflector.

"One short hour sufficed to prove the utter uselessness of our efforts. The storm barricaded the track with a dozen drifts while we dug one away. And worse than this, it was discovered that the last grand charge the engine had made upon the enemy had broken the fore-and-aft shaft of the driving-wheel! With a free track before us we should still have been helpless. We entered the car wearied with labor, and very sorrowful. We gathered about the stoves, and gravely canvassed our situation. We had no provisions whatever—in this lay our chief distress. We could not freeze, for there was a good supply of wood in the tender. This was our only comfort. The discussion ended at last in accepting the disheartening decision of the conductor, viz., that it would be death for any man to attempt to travel fifty miles on foot through snow like that. We could not send for help; and even if we could, it could not come. We must submit, and await, as patiently as we might, succor or starvation! I think the stoutest heart there felt a momentary chill when those words were uttered.

"Within the hour conversation subsided to a low murmur here and there about the car, caught fitfully between the rising and falling of the blast; the lamps grew dim; and the majority of the castaways settled themselves among the flickering shadows to think—to forget the present, if they could—to sleep, if they might.

"The eternal night—it surely seemed eternal to us—wore its lagging hours away at last, and the cold grey dawn broke in the east. As the light grew stronger the passengers began to stir and give signs of life, one after another, and each in turn pushed his slouched hat up from his forehead, stretched his stiffened limbs, and glanced out at the windows upon the cheerless prospect. It was cheerless indeed!—not a living thing visible anywhere, not a human habitation; nothing but a vast white desert; uplifted sheets of snow drifting hither and thither before the wind—a world of eddying flakes shutting out the firmament above.

"All day we moped about the cars, saying little, thinking much. Another lingering dreary night—and hunger.

"Another dawning—another day of silence, sadness, wasting hunger, hopeless watching for succor that could not come. A night of restless slumber, filled with dreams of feasting—wakings distressed with the gnawings of hunger.

"The fourth day came and went—and the fifth! Five days of dreadful imprisonment! A savage hunger looked out at every eye. There was in it a sign of awful import —the foreshadowing of a something that was vaguely shaping itself in every heart—a something which no tongue dared yet to frame into words.

"The sixth day passed—the seventh dawned upon as gaunt and haggard and hopeless a company of men as ever stood in the shadow of death. It must out now! That thing which had been growing up in every heart was ready to leap from every lip at last! Nature had been taxed to the utmost—she must yield. RICHARD H. GASTON, of Minnesota, tall, cadaverous, and pale, rose up. All knew what was coming. All prepared—every emotion, every semblance of excitement was smothered —only a calm, thoughtful seriousness appeared in the eyes that were lately so wild.

"'Gentlemen,—It cannot be delayed longer! The time is at hand! We must determine which of us shall die to furnish food for the rest!'

"Mr. JOHN J. WILLIAMS, of Illinois, rose and said: 'Gentlemen,—I nominate the Rev. James Sawyer, of Tennessee.'

"Mr. WM. R. ADAMS, of Indiana, said: 'I nominate Mr. Daniel Slote, of New York.'

"Mr. CHARLES J. LANGDON: 'I nominate Mr. Samuel A. Bowen, of St. Louis.'

"Mr: SLOTE: 'Gentlemen,—I desire to decline in favor of Mr. John A. Van Nostrand, Jun., of New Jersey.'

"Mr. GASTON: 'If there be no objection, the gentleman's desire will be acceded to.'

"Mr. VAN NOSTRAND objecting, the resignation of Mr. Slote was rejected. The resignations of Messrs. Sawyer and Bowen were also offered, and refused upon the same grounds.

"Mr. A. L. BASCOM, of Ohio: 'I move that the nominations now close, and that the House proceed to an election by ballot.'

"Mr. SAWYER: 'Gentlemen,—I protest earnestly against these proceedings. They are, in every way, irregular and unbecoming. I must beg to move that they be dropped at once, and that we elect a chairman of the meeting and proper officers to assist him, and then we can go on with the business before us understandingly.'

"Mr. BELL, of Iowa: 'Gentlemen,—I object. This is no time to stand upon forms and ceremonious observances. For more than seven days we have been without food. Every moment we lose in idle discussion increases our distress. I am satisfied with the nominations that have been made—every gentleman present is, I believe—and I, for one, do not see why we should not proceed at once to elect one or more of them. I wish to offer a resolution—'

"Mr. GASTON: 'It would be objected to, and have to lie over one day under the rules, thus bringing about the very delay you wish to avoid. The gentleman from New Jersey—'

"Mr. VAN NOSTRAND: 'Gentlemen,—I am a stranger among you; I have not sought the distinction that has been conferred upon me, and I feel a delicacy—'

"Mr. MORGAN, of Alabama (interrupting): 'I move the previous question.'

"The motion was carried, and further debate shut off, of course. The motion to elect officers was passed, and under it Mr. Gaston was chosen chairman, Mr. Blake secretary, Messrs. Holcomb, Dyer, and Baldwin, a committee on nominations, and Mr. R. M. Howland, purveyor, to assist the committee in making selections.

"A recess of half an hour was then taken, and some little caucussing followed. At the sound of the gavel the meeting reassembled, and the committee reported in favor of Messrs. George Ferguson, of Kentucky, Lucien Herrman, of Louisiana, and W. Messick, of Colorado, as candidates. The report was accepted.

"Mr. ROGERS, of Missouri: 'Mr. President,—The report being properly before the House now, I move to amend it by substituting for the name of Mr. Herman that of Mr. Lucius Harris, of St. Louis, who is well and honorably known to us all. I do not wish to be understood as casting the least reflection upon the high character and standing of the gentleman from Louisiana—far from it. I respect and esteem him as much as any gentleman here present possibly can; but none of us can be blind to the fact that he has lost more flesh during the week that we have lain here than any among us—none of us can be blind to the fact that the committee has been derelict in its duty, either through negligence or a graver fault, in thus offering for our suffrages a gentleman who, however pure his own motives may be, has really less nutriment in him—'

"The CHAIR: 'The gentleman from Missouri will take his seat. The Chair cannot allow the integrity of the Committee to be questioned save by the regular course, under the rules. What action will the House take upon the gentleman's motion?'

"Mr. HALLIDAY, of Virginia: 'I move to further amend the report by substituting Mr. Harvey Davis, of Oregon, for Mr. Messick. It may be urged by gentlemen that the hardships and privations of a frontier life have rendered Mr. Davis tough; but, gentlemen, is this a time to cavil at toughness? is this a time to be fastidious concerning trifles? is this a time to dispute about matters of paltry significance? No, gentlemen, bulk is what we desire—substance, weight, bulk—these are the supreme requisites now—not talent, not genius, not education. I insist upon my motion.'

"Mr. MORGAN (excitedly): 'Mr. Chairman,—I do most strenuously object to this amendment. The gentleman from Oregon is old, and furthermore is bulky only in bone—not in flesh. I ask the gentleman from Virginia if it is soup we want instead of solid sustenance? if he would delude us with shadows? if he would mock our suffering with an Oregonian spectre? I ask him if he can look upon the anxious faces around him, if he can gaze into our sad eyes, if he can listen to the beating of our expectant hearts, and still thrust this famine-stricken fraud upon us? I ask him if he can think of our desolate state, of our past sorrows, of our dark future, and still unpityingly foist upon us this wreck, this ruin, this tottering swindle, this gnarled and blighted and sapless vagabond from Oregon's inhospitable shores? Never!' (Applause.)

"The amendment was put to vote, after a fiery debate, and lost. Mr. Harris was substituted on the first amendment. The balloting then began. Five ballots were held without a choice. On the sixth, Mr. Harris was elected, all voting for him but himself. It was then moved that his election should be ratified by acclamation, which was lost, in consequence of his again voting against himself.

"Mr. RADWAY moved that the House now take up the remaining candidates, and go into an election for breakfast. This was carried.

"On the first ballot there was a tie, half the members favoring one candidate on account of his youth, and half favoring the other on account of his superior size. The President gave the casting vote for the latter, Mr. Messick. This decision created considerable dissatisfaction among the friends of Mr. Ferguson, the defeated candidate, and there was some talk of demanding a new ballot; but in the midst of it, a motion to adjourn was carried, and the meeting broke up at once.

"The preparations for supper diverted the attention of the Ferguson faction from the discussion of their grievance for a long time, and then, when they would have taken it up again, the happy announcement that Mr. Harris was ready, drove all thought of it to the winds.

"We improvised tables by propping up the backs of car-seats, and sat down with hearts full of gratitude to the finest supper that had blessed our vision for seven torturing days. How changed we were from what we had been a few short hours before! Hopeless, sad-eyed misery, hunger, feverish anxiety, desperation, then—thankfulness, serenity, joy too deep for utterance now. That I know was the cheeriest hour of my eventful life. The wind howled, and blew the snow wildly about our prison-house, but they were powerless to distress us any more. I liked Harris. He might have been better done, perhaps, but I am free to say that no man ever agreed with me better than Harris, or afforded me so large a degree of satisfaction. Messick was very well, though rather high-flavored, but for genuine nutritiousness and delicacy of fibre, give me Harris. Messick had his good points—I will not attempt to deny it, nor do I wish to do it—but he was no more fitted for breakfast than a mummy would be, sir—not a bit. Lean?—why, bless me!—and tough? Ah, he was very tough! You could not imagine it,—you could never imagine anything like it."

"Do you mean to tell me that—"

"Do not interrupt me, please. After breakfast we elected a man by the name of Walker, from Detroit, for supper. He was very good. I wrote his wife so afterwards. He was worthy of all praise. I shall always remember Walker. He was a little rare, but very good. And then the next morning we had Morgan, of Alabama, for breakfast. He was one of the finest men I ever sat down to,—handsome educated, refined, spoke several languages fluently—a perfect gentleman—he was a perfect gentleman, and singularly juicy. For supper we had that Oregon patriarch, and he *was* a fraud, there is no question about it—old, scraggy, tough, nobody can picture the reality. I finally said, gentlemen, you can do as you like, but *I* will wait for another election. And Grimes, of Illinois, said, 'Gentlemen, *I* will wait also. When you elect a man that has *something* to recommend him, I shall be glad to join you again.' It soon became evident that there was general dissatisfaction with Davis, of Oregon, and so, to preserve the good-will that had prevailed so pleasantly since we had had Harris, an election was called, and the result of it was that Baker, of Georgia, was chosen. He was splendid! Well, well—after that we had Doolittle and Hawkins, and McElroy (there was some complaint about McElroy, because he was uncommonly short and thin), and Penrod, and two Smiths, and Bailey (Bailey had a wooden leg, which was clear loss, but he was otherwise good), and an Indian boy, and an organ grinder, and a gentleman by the name of Buckminster —a poor stick of a vagabond that wasn't any good for company and no account for breakfast. We were glad we got him elected before relief came."

"And so the blessed relief *did* come at last?"

"Yes, it came one bright, sunny morning, just after election. John Murphy was the choice, and there never was a better, I am willing to testify; but John Murphy came home with us, in the train that came to succor us, and lived to marry the widow Harris—"

" Relict of—"

"Relict of our first choice. He married her, and is happy and respected and prosperous yet. Ah, it was like a novel, sir—it was like a romance. This is my stopping-place, sir; I must bid you good-by. Any time that you can make it convenient to tarry a day or two with me, I shall be glad to have you. I like you, sir; I have conceived an affection for you. I could like you as well as I liked Harris himself, sir. Good day, sir, and a pleasant journey."

He was gone. I never felt so stunned, so distressed, so bewildered in my life. But in my soul I was glad he was gone. With all his gentleness of manner and his soft voice, I shuddered whenever he turned his hungry eye upon me; and when I heard that I had achieved his perilous affection, and that I stood almost with the late Harris in his esteem, my heart fairly stood still!

I was bewildered beyond description. I did not doubt his word; I could not question a single item in a statement so stamped with the earnestness of truth as his; but its dreadful details overpowered me, and threw my thoughts into hopeless confusion. I saw the conductor looking at me. I said, "Who is that man?"

"He was a member of Congress once, and a good one. But he got caught in a snowdrift in the cars, and like to been starved to death. He got so frost-bitten and frozen up generally, and used up for want of something to eat, that he was sick and out of his head two or three months afterwards. He is all right now, only he is a monomaniac, and when he gets on that old subject he never stops till he has eat up that whole car-load of people he talks about. He would have finished the crowd by this time, only he had to get out here. He has got their names as pat as A, B, C. When he gets them all eat up but himself, he always says:—'Then the hour for the usual election for breakfast having arrived, and there being no opposition, I was duly elected, after which, there being no objections offered, I resigned. Thus I am here.'"

I felt inexpressibly relieved to know that I had only been listening to the harmless vagaries of a madman instead of the genuine experiences of a bloodthirsty cannibal.

1868

A Fine Old Man

JOHN WAGNER, the oldest man in Buffalo—one hundred and four years old—recently walked a mile and a half in two weeks.

He is as cheerful and bright as any of these other old men that charge around so persistently and tiresomely in the newspapers, and in every way as remarkable.

Last November he walked five blocks in a rainstorm, without any shelter but an umbrella, and cast his vote for Grant, remarking that he had voted for forty-seven presidents—which was a lie.

His "second crop" of rich brown hair arrived from New York yesterday, and he has a new set of teeth coming—from Philadelphia.

He is to be married next week to a girl one hundred and two years old, who still takes in washing.

They have been engaged eighty years, but their parents persistently refused their consent until three days ago.

John Wagner is two years older than the Rhode Island veteran, and yet has never tasted a drop of liquor in his life—unless—unless you count whisky.

1869

A Visit to Niagara

NIAGARA FALLS is a most enjoyable place of resort. The hotels are excellent, and the prices not at all exorbitant. The opportunities for fishing are not surpassed in the country; in fact, they are not even equalled elsewhere. Because, in other localities, certain places in the streams are much better than others; but at Niagara one place is just as good as another, for the reason that the fish do not bite anywhere, and so there is no use in your walking five miles to fish, when you can depend on being just as unsuccessful nearer home. The advantages of this state of things have never heretofore been properly placed before the public.

The weather is cool in summer, and the walks and drives are all pleasant and none of them fatiguing. When you start out to "do" the Falls you first drive down about a mile, and pay a small sum for the privilege of looking down from a precipice into the narrowest part of the Niagara river. A railway "cut" through a hill would be as comely if it had the angry river tumbling and foaming through its bottom. You can descend a staircase here a hundred and fifty feet down, and stand at the edge of the water. After you have done it, you will wonder why you did it; but you will then be too late.

The guide will explain to you, in his blood-curdling

way, how he saw the little steamer, *Maid of the Mist*, descend the fearful rapids—how first one paddle-box was out of sight behind the raging billows, and then the other, and at what point it was that her smokestack toppled overboard, and where her planking began to break and part asunder—and how she did finally live through the trip, after accomplishing the incredible feat of travelling seventeen miles in six minutes, or six miles in seventeen minutes, I have really forgotten which. But it was very extraordinary, anyhow. It is worth the price of admission to hear the guide tell the story nine times in succession to different parties, and never miss a word or alter a sentence or a gesture.

Then you drive over the Suspension Bridge, and divide your misery between the chances of smashing down two hundred feet into the river below, and the chances of having the railway train overhead smashing down on to you. Either possibility is discomforting taken by itself, but mixed together, they amount in the aggregate to positive unhappiness.

On the Canada side you drive along the chasm between long ranks of photographers standing guard behind their cameras, ready to make an ostentatious frontispiece of you and your decaying ambulance, and your solemn crate with a hide on it, which you are expected to regard in the light of a horse, and a diminished and unimportant background of sublime Niagara; and a great many people *have* the incredible effrontery or the native depravity to aid and abet this sort of crime.

Any day, in the hands of these photographers, you may see stately pictures of papa and mamma, Johnny and Bub and Sis, or a couple of country cousins, all smiling vacantly, and all disposed in studied and uncomfortable attitudes in their carriage, and all looming up in their awe-inspiring imbecility before the snubbed and diminished presentment of that majestic presence whose ministering spirits are the rainbows, whose voice is the thunder, whose awful front is veiled in clouds, who was monarch here dead and forgotten ages before this hackful of small reptiles was deemed temporarily necessary to fill a crack in the world's unnoted myriads, and will still be monarch here ages and decades of ages after they shall have gathered themselves to their blood relations, the other worms, and been mingled with the unremembering dust.

There is no actual harm in making Niagara a background whereon to display one's marvellous insignificance in a good strong light, but it requires a sort of superhuman self-complacency to enable one to do it.

When you have examined the stupendous Horseshoe Fall till you are satisfied you cannot improve on it, you return to America by the new Suspension Bridge, and follow up the bank to where they exhibit the Cave of the Winds.

Here I followed instructions, and divested myself of all my clothing, and put on a waterproof jacket and overalls. This costume is picturesque, but not beautiful. A guide, similarly dressed, led the way down a flight of winding stairs, which wound and wound, and still kept on winding long after the thing ceased to be a novelty, and then terminated long before it had begun to be a pleasure. We were then well down under the precipice, but still considerably above the level of the river.

We now began to creep along flimsy bridges of a single plank, our persons shielded from destruction by a crazy wooden railing, to which I clung with both hands—not because I was afraid, but because I wanted to. Presently the descent became steeper, and the bridge flimsier, and sprays from the American Fall began to rain down on us in fast-increasing sheets that soon became blinding, and after that our progress was mostly in the nature of groping. Now a furious wind began to rush out from behind the waterfall, which seemed determined to sweep us from the bridge, and scatter us on the rocks and among the torrents below. I remarked that I wanted to go home; but it was too late. We were almost under the monstrous wall of water thundering down from above, and speech was in vain in the midst of such a pitiless crash of sound.

In another moment the guide disappeared behind the deluge, and bewildered by the thunder, driven helplessly by the wind, and smitten by the arrowy tempest of rain, I followed. All was darkness. Such a mad storming, roaring, and bellowing of warring wind and water never crazed my ears before. I bent my head, and seemed to receive the Atlantic on my back. The world seemed going to destruction. I could not see anything, the flood poured down so savagely. I raised my head, with open mouth, and the most of the American cataract went down my throat. If I had sprung a leak now, I had been lost. And at this moment I discovered that the bridge had ceased, and we must trust for a foothold to the slippery and precipitous rocks. I never was so scared before and survived it. But we got through at last, and emerged into the open day, where we could stand in front of the laced and frothy and seething world of descending water, and look at it. When I saw how much of it there was, and how fearfully in earnest it was, I was sorry I had gone behind it.

The noble Red Man has always been a friend and darling of mine. I love to read about him in tales and legends and romances. I love to read of his inspired sagacity, and his love of the wild free life of mountain and forest, and his general nobility of character, and his stately metaphorical manner of speech, and his chivalrous love for the dusky maiden, and the picturesque pomp of his dress and accoutrements. Especially the picturesque pomp of his dress and accoutrements. When I found the shops at Niagara Falls full of dainty Indian bead-work, and stunning moccasins, and equally stunning toy figures representing human beings who carried their weapons in holes bored through their arms and bodies, and had feet shaped like a pie, I was filled with emotion. I knew that now, at last, I was going to come face to face with the noble Red Man.

A lady clerk in a shop told me, indeed, that all her grand array of curiosities were made by the Indians, and that they were plenty about the Falls, and that they were friendly, and it would not be dangerous to speak to them. And sure enough, as I approached the bridge leading over to Luna Island, I came upon a noble Son of the Forest sitting under a tree, diligently at work on a bead reticule. He wore a slouch hat and brogans, and had a short black pipe in his mouth. Thus does the baneful contact with our effeminate civilization dilute the picturesque pomp which is so natural to the Indian when far removed from us in his native haunts. I addressed the relic as follows:—

"Is the Wawhoo-Wang-Wang of the Whack-a-Whack happy? Does the great Speckled Thunder sigh for the war path, or is his heart contented with dreaming of the dusky maiden, the Pride of the Forest? Does the mighty Sachem yearn to drink the blood of his enemies, or is he satisfied to make bead reticules for the pappooses of the paleface? Speak, sublime relic of bygone grandeur—venerable ruin, speak!"

The relic said—

"An' is it mesilf, Dennis Hooligan, that ye'd be takin' for a dirty Injin, ye drawlin', lantern-jawed, spider-legged divil! By the piper that played before Moses, I'll ate ye!"

I went away from there.

By and by, in the neighborhood of the Terrapin Tower, I came upon a gentle daughter of the aborigines in fringed and beaded buckskin moccasins and leggins, seated on a bench, with her pretty wares about her. She had just carved out a wooden chief that had a strong family resemblance to a clothes-pin, and was now boring a hole through his abdomen to put his bow through. I hesitated a moment, and then addressed her:

"Is the heart of the forest maiden heavy? Is the Laughing Tadpole lonely? Does she mourn over the extinguished council-fires of her race, and the vanished glory of her ancestors? Or does her sad spirit wander afar toward the hunting grounds whither her brave Gobbler-of-the-Lightnings is gone? Why is my daughter silent? Has she aught against the paleface stranger?"

The maiden said—

"Faix, an' is it Biddy Malone ye dare to be callin' names? Lave this, or I'll shy your lean carcass over the cataract, ye sniveling blaggard!"

I adjourned from there also.

"Confound these Indians!" I said. "They told me they were tame; but, if appearances go for anything, I should say they were all on the war path."

I made one more attempt to fraternize with them, and only one. I came upon a camp of them gathered in the shade of a great tree, making wampum and moccasins, and addressed them in the language of friendship:

"Noble Red Men, Braves, Grand Sachems, War Chiefs, Squaws, and High Muck-a-Mucks, the paleface from the land of the setting sun greets you! You, Beneficent Polecat—you, Devourer of Mountains—you, Roaring Thundergust—you, Bully Boy with a Glass eye—the paleface from beyond the great waters greets you all! War and pestilence have thinned your ranks, and destroyed your once proud nation. Poker and seven-up, and a vain modern expense for soap, unknown to your glorious ancestors, have depleted your purses. Appropriating, in your simplicity, the property of others, has gotten you into trouble. Misrepresenting facts, in your simple innocence, has damaged your reputation with the soulless usurper. Trading for forty-rod whisky, to enable you to get drunk and happy and tomahawk your families, has played the everlasting mischief with the picturesque pomp of your dress, and here you are, in the broad light of the nineteenth century, gotten up like the ragtag and bobtail of the purlieus of New York. For shame! Remember your ancestors! Recall their mighty deeds! Remember Uncas!—and Red Jacket!—and Hole in the Day!—and Whoopdedoodledo! Emulate their achievements! Unfurl yourselves under my banner, noble savages, illustrious guttersnipes"—

"Down wid him!" "Scoop the blaggard!" "Burn him!" "Hang him!" "Dhround him!"

It was the quickest operation that ever was. I simply saw a sudden flash in the air of clubs, brickbats, fists, bead-baskets, and moccasins—a single flash, and they all appeared to hit me at once, and no two of them in the same place. In the next instant the entire tribe was upon me. They tore half the clothes off me; they broke my arms and legs; they gave me a thump that dented the top of my head till it would hold coffee like a saucer; and, to crown their disgraceful proceedings and add insult to injury, they threw me over the Niagara Falls, and I got wet.

About ninety or a hundred feet from the top, the remains of my vest caught on a projecting rock, and I was almost drowned before I could get loose. I finally fell, and brought up in a world of white foam at the foot of the Fall, whose celled and bubbly masses towered up several inches above my head. Of course I got into the eddy. I sailed round and round in it forty-four times—chasing a chip and gaining on it—each round trip a half mile—reaching for the same bush on the bank forty-four times, and just exactly missing it by a hair's-breadth every time.

At last a man walked down and sat down close to that bush, and put a pipe in his mouth, and lit a match, and followed me with one eye and kept the other on the match, while he sheltered it in his hands from the wind. Presently a puff of wind blew it out. The next time I swept around he said—

"Got a match?"

"Yes; in my other vest. Help me out, please."

"Not for Joe."

When I came round again, I said—

"Excuse the seemingly impertinent curiosity of a drowning man, but will you explain this singular conduct of yours?"

"With pleasure. I am the coroner. Don't hurry on my account. I can wait for you. But I wish I had a match."

I said— "Take my place, and I'll go and get you one."

He declined. This lack of confidence on his part created a coldness between us, and from that time forward I avoided him. It was my idea, in case anything happened to me, to so time the occurrence as to throw my custom into the hands of the opposition coroner over on the American side.

At last a policeman came along, and arrested me for disturbing the peace by yelling at people on shore for help. The judge fined me, but I had the advantage of him. My money was with my pantaloons, and my pantaloons were with the Indians.

Thus I escaped. I am now lying in a very critical condition. At least I am lying anyway—critical or not critical. I am hurt all over, but I cannot tell the full extent yet, because the doctor is not done taking inventory. He will make out my manifest this evening. However, thus far he thinks only sixteen of my wounds are fatal. I don't mind the others.

Upon regaining my right mind, I said—

"It is an awful savage tribe of Indians that do the bead work and moccasins for Niagara Falls, doctor. Where are they from?"

"Limerick, my son."

1869

The Personal Habits of the Siamese Twins

I DO not wish to write of the personal *habits* of these strange creatures solely, but also of certain curious details of various kinds concerning them, which belonging only to their private life, have never crept into print. Knowing the Twins intimately, I feel that I am peculiarly well qualified for the task I have taken upon myself.

The Siamese Twins are naturally tender and affectionate in disposition, and have clung to each other with singular fidelity throughout a long and eventful life. Even as children they were inseparable companions; and it was noticed that they always seemed to prefer each other's society to that of any other persons. They nearly always played together; and, so accustomed was their mother to this peculiarity, that, whenever both of them chanced to be lost, she usually only hunted for one of them—satisfied that when she found that one she would find his brother somewhere in the immediate neighborhood. And yet these creatures were ignorant and unlettered—barbarians themselves and the offspring of barbarians, who knew not the light of philosophy and science. What a withering rebuke is this to our boasted civilization, with its quarrelings, its wranglings, and its separations of brothers!

As men, the Twins have not always lived in perfect accord; but still there has always been a bond between them which made them unwilling to go away from each other and dwell apart. They have even occupied the same house, as a general thing, and it is believed that they have never failed to even sleep together on any night since they were born. How surely do the habits of a lifetime become second nature to us! The Twins always go to bed at the same time; but Chang usually gets up about an hour before his brother. By an understanding between themselves, Chang does all the in-door work and Eng runs all the errands. This is because Eng likes to go out; Chang's habits are sedentary. However, Chang always goes along. Eng is a Baptist, but Chang is a Roman Catholic; still, to please his brother, Chang consented to be baptized at the same time that Eng was, on condition that it should not "count." During the War they were strong partizans, and both fought gallantly all through the great struggle—Eng on the Union side and Chang on the Confederate. They took each other prisoners at Seven Oaks, but the proofs of capture were so evenly balanced in favor of each, that a general army court had to be assembled to determine which one was properly the captor, and which the captive. The jury was unable to agree for a long time; but the vexed question was finally decided by agreeing to consider them both prisoners, and then exchanging them. At one time Chang was convicted of disobedience of orders, and sentenced to ten days in the guard-house, but Eng, in spite of all arguments, felt obliged to share his imprisonment, notwithstanding he himself was entirely innocent; and so, to save the blameless brother from suffering, they had to discharge both from custody—the just reward of faithfulness.

Upon one occasion the brothers fell out about something, and Chang knocked Eng down, and then tripped and fell on him, whereupon both clinched and began to beat and gouge each other without mercy. The bystanders interferred, and tried to separate them, but they could not do it, and so allowed them to fight it out. In the end both were disabled, and were carried to the hospital on one and the same shutter.

Their ancient habit of going always together had its drawbacks when they reached man's estate, and entered upon the luxury of courting. Both fell in love with the same girl. Each tried to steal clandestine interviews with her, but at the critical moment the other would always turn up. By and by Eng saw, with distraction, that Chang had won the girl's affections; and, from that day forth, he had to bear with the agony of being a witness to all their dainty billing and cooing. But with a magnanimity that did him infinite credit, he succumbed to his fate, and gave countenance and encouragement to a state of things that bade fair to sunder his generous heart-strings. He sat from seven every evening until two in the morning, listening to the fond foolishness of the two lovers, and to the concussion of hundreds of squandered kisses—for the privilege of sharing only one of which he would have given his right hand. But he sat patiently, and waited, and gaped, and yawned, and stretched, and longed for two o'clock to come. And he took long walks with the lovers on moonlight evenings—sometimes traversing ten miles, notwithstanding he was usually suffering from rheumatism. He is an inveterate smoker; but he could not smoke on these occasions, because the young lady was painfully sensitive to the smell of tobacco. Eng cordially wanted them married, and done with it; but although Chang often asked the momentous question, the young lady could not gather sufficient courage to answer it while Eng was by. However, on one occasion, after having walked some sixteen miles, and sat up till nearly daylight, Eng dropped asleep, from sheer exhaustion, and then the question was asked and answered. The lovers were married. All acquainted with the circumstance applauded the noble brother-in-law. His unwavering faithfulness was the theme of every tongue. He had stayed by them all through their long and arduous courtship; and when at last they were married, he lifted his hands above their heads, and said with impressive unction, "Bless ye, my children I will never desert ye!" and he kept his word. Fidelity like this is all too rare in this cold world.

By and by Eng fell in love with his sister-in-law's sister, and married her, and since that day they have all lived together, night and day, in an exceeding sociability which is touching and beautiful to behold, and is a scathing rebuke to our boasted civilization.

The sympathy existing between these two brothers is so close and so refined that the feelings, the impulses, the emotions of the one are instantly experienced by the other. When one is sick, the other is sick; when one feels pain, the other feels it; when one is angered, the other's temper takes fire. We have already seen with what happy facility they both fell in love with the same girl. Now, Chang is bitterly opposed to all forms of intemperance, on principle; but Eng is the reverse—for, while these men's feelings and emotion are so closely wedded, their reasoning faculties are unfettered; their *thoughts* are free. Chang belongs to the Good Templars, and is a hard working, enthusiastic supporter of all temperance reforms. But, to his bitter distress, every now and then Eng gets drunk, and, of course, that makes Chang drunk too. This unfortunate thing has been a great sorrow to Chang, for it almost destroys his usefulness in his favorite field of effort. As sure as he is to head a great temperance procession Eng ranges up alongside of him, prompt to the minute, and drunk as a lord; but yet no more dismally and hopelessly drunk than his brother, who has not tasted a drop. And so the two begin to hoot and yell, and throw mud and bricks at the Good Templars; and of course they break up the procession. It would be manifestly wrong to punish Chang for what Eng does, and, therefore, the Good Templars accept the untoward situation, and suffer in silence and sorrow. They have officially and deliberately examined into the matter, and find Chang blameless. They have taken the two brothers and filled Chang full of warm water and sugar and Eng full of whisky, and in twenty-five minutes it was not possible to tell which was the drunkest. Both were as drunk as loons—and on hot whisky punches, by the smell of their breath. Yet all the while Chang's moral principles were unsullied, his conscience clear; and so all just men were forced to confess that he was not morally, but only physically drunk. By every right and by every moral evidence the man was strictly sober; and, therefore, it caused his friends all the more anguish to see him shake hands with the pump, and try to wind his watch with his night-key.

There is a moral in these solemn warnings—or, at least, a warning in these solemn morals; one or the other. No matter, it is somehow. Let us heed it; let us profit by it.

I could say more of an instructive nature about these interesting beings, but let what I have written suffice.

Having forgotton to mention it sooner, I will remark in conclusion, that the ages of the Siamese Twins are respectively fifty-one and fifty-three years.

1869

Journalism in Tennessee

The editor of the Memphis *Avalanche* swoops thus mildly down upon a correspondent who posted him as a Radical:— "While he was writing the first word, the middle, dotting his i's, crossing his t's, and punching his period, he knew he was concocting a sentence that was saturated with infamy and reeking with falsehood."—*Exchange*.

I WAS told by the physician that a Southern climate would improve my health, and so I went down to Tennessee, and got a berth on the *Morning Glory and Johnson County War-Whoop* as associate editor. When I went on duty I found the chief editor sitting tilted back in a three-legged chair with his feet on a pine table. There was another pine table in the room and another afflicted chair, and both were half buried under newspapers and scraps and sheets of manuscript. There was a wooden box of sand, sprinkled with cigar stubs and "old soldiers," and a stove with a door hanging by its upper hinge. The chief editor had a long-tailed black cloth frock coat on, and white linen pants. His boots were small and neatly blacked. He wore a ruffled shirt, a large seal ring, a standing collar of obsolete pattern, and a checkered neckerchief with the ends hanging down. Date of costume about 1848. He was smoking a cigar, and trying to think of a word, and in pawing his hair he had rumpled his locks a good deal. He was scowling fearfully, and I judged that he was concocting a particularly knotty editorial. He told me to take the exchanges and skim through them and write up the "Spirit of the Tennessee Press," condensing into the article all of their contents that seemed of interest.

I wrote as follows:—

"SPIRIT OF THE TENNESSEE PRESS.

"The editors of the *Semi-Weekly Earthquake* evidently labor under a misapprehension with regard to the Ballyhack railroad. It is not the object of the company to leave Buzzardville off to one side. On the contrary, they consider it one of the most important points along the line, and consequently can have no desire to slight it. The gentlemen of the *Earthquake* will, of course, take pleasure in making the correction.

"John W. Blossom, Esq., the able editor of the Higginsville *Thunderbolt and Battle Cry of Freedom*, arrived in the city yesterday. He is stopping at the Van Buren House.

"We observe that our contemporary of the Mud Springs *Morning Howl* has fallen into the error of supposing that the election of Van Werter is not an established fact, but he will have discovered his mistake before this reminder reaches him, no doubt. He was doubtless misled by incomplete election returns.

"It is pleasant to note that the city of Blathersville is endeavoring to contract with some New York gentlemen to pave its well-nigh impassable streets with the Nicholson pavement. The *Daily Hurrah* urges the measure with ability, and seems confident of ultimate success."

I passed my manuscript over to the chief editor for acceptance, alteration, or destruction. He glanced at it and his face clouded. He ran his eye down the pages, and his countenance grew portentous. It was easy to see that something was wrong. Presently he sprang up and said—

"Thunder and lightning! Do you suppose I am going to speak of those cattle that way? Do you suppose my subscribers are going to stand such gruel as that? Give me the pen!"

I never saw a pen scrape and scratch its way so viciously, or plough through another man's verbs and adjectives so relentlessly. While he was in the midst of his work, somebody shot at him through the open window, and marred the symmetry of my ear.

"Ah," said he, " that is that scoundrel Smith, of the *Moral Volcano*—he was due yesterday." And he snatched a navy revolver from his belt and fired. Smith dropped, shot in the thigh. The shot spoiled Smith's aim, who was just taking a second chance, and he crippled a stranger. It was me. Merely a finger shot off.

Then the chief editor went on with his erasures and interlineations. Just as he finished them a hand-grenade came down the stove-pipe, and the explosion shivered the stove into a thousand fragments. However, it did no further damage, except that a vagrant piece knocked a couple of my teeth out.

"That stove is utterly ruined," said the chief editor.

I said I believed it was.

"Well, no matter—don't want it this kind of weather. I know the man that did it. I'll get him. Now, *here* is the way this stuff ought to be written."

I took the manuscript. It was scarred with erasures and interlineations till its mother wouldn't have known it if it had had one. It now read as follows:—

"SPIRIT OF THE TENNESSEE PRESS.

"The inveterate liars of the *Semi-Weekly Earthquake* are

evidently endeavoring to palm off upon a noble and chivalrous people another of their vile and brutal falsehoods with regard to that most glorious conception of the nineteenth century, the Ballyhack railroad. The idea that Buzzardville was to be left off at one side originated in their own fulsome brains—or rather in the settlings which *they* regard as brains. They had better swallow this lie if they want to save their abandoned reptile carcasses the cowhiding they so richly deserve.

"That ass, Blossom, of the Higginsville *Thunderbolt and Battle Cry of Freedom*, is down here again sponging at the Van Buren.

"We observe that the besotted blackguard of the Mud Spring *Morning Howl* is giving out, with his usual propensity for lying, that Van Werter is not elected. The heaven-born mission of journalism is to disseminate truth; to eradicate error; to educate, refine, and elevate the tone of public morals and manners, and make all men more gentle, more virtuous, more charitable, and in all ways better, and holier, and happier; and yet this black-hearted scoundrel degrades his great office persistently to the dissemination of falsehood, calumny, vituperation, and vulgarity.

"Blathersville wants a Nicholson pavement—it wants a jail and a poorhouse more. The idea of a pavement in a one horse town composed of two gin mills, a blacksmith's shop, and that mustard-plaster of a newspaper, the *Daily Hurrah*! The crawling insect, Buckner, who edits the *Hurrah*, is braying about this business with his customary imbecility, and imagining that he is talking sense."

"Now *that* is the way to write—peppery and to the point. Mush-and-milk journalism gives me the fantods."

About this time a brick came through the window with a splintering crash, and gave me a considerable jolt in the back. I moved out of range—I began to feel in the way.

The chief said, "That was the Colonel, likely. I've been expecting him for two days. He will be up, now, right away."

He was correct. The Colonel appeared in the door a moment afterward with a dragoon revolver in his hand.

He said, "Sir, have I the honor of addressing the poltroon who edits this mangy sheet?"

"You have. Be seated, sir. Be careful of the chair, one of its legs is gone. I believe I have the honor of addressing the putrid liar, Col. Blatherskite Tecumseh?"

"Right, sir. I have a little account to settle with you. If you are at leisure we will begin."

"I have an article on the 'Encouraging Progress of Moral and Intellectual Development in America' to finish, but there is no hurry. Begin."

Both pistols rang out their fierce clamor at the same instant. The chief lost a lock of his hair, and the Colonel's bullet ended its career in the fleshy part of my thigh. The Colonel's left shoulder was clipped a little. They fired again. Both missed their men this time, but I got my share, a shot in the arm. At the third fire both gentleman were wounded slightly, and I had a knuckle chipped. I then said, I believed I would go out and take a walk, as this was a private matter, and I had a delicacy about participating in it further. But both gentlemen begged me to keep my seat, and assured me that I was not in the way.

They then talked about the elections and the crops while they reloaded, and I fell to tying up my wounds. But presently they opened fire again with animation, and every shot took effect—but it is proper to remark that five out of the six fell to my share. The sixth one mortally wounded the Colonel, who remarked, with fine humor, that he would have to say good morning now, as he had business up town. He then inquired the way to the undertaker's and left.

The chief turned to me and said, "I am expecting company to dinner, and shall have to get ready. It will be a favor to me if you will read proof and attend to the customers."

I winced a little at the idea of attending to the customers, but I was too bewildered by the fusilade that was still ringing in my ears to think of anything to say.

He continued, "Jones will be here at 3—cowhide him. Gillespie will call earlier, perhaps—throw him out of the window. Ferguson will be along about 4—kill him. That is all for to-day, I believe. If you have any odd time, you may write a blistering article on the police—give the Chief Inspector rats. The cowhides are under the table; weapons in the drawer—ammunition there in the corner—lint and bandages up there in the pigeon-holes. In case of accident, go to Lancet, the surgeon, down-stairs. He advertises—we take it out in trade."

He was gone. I shuddered. At the end of the next three hours I had been through perils so awful that all peace of mind and all cheerfulness were gone from me. Gillespie had called and thrown *me* out of the window. Jones arrived promptly, and when I got ready to do the cowhiding he took the job off my hands. In an encounter with a stranger, not in the bill of fare, I had lost my scalp. Another stranger, by the name of Thompson, left me a mere wreck and ruin of chaotic rags. And at last, at bay in the corner, and beset by an infuriated mob of editors, blacklegs, politicians, and desperadoes, who raved and swore and flourished their weapons about my head till the air shimmered with glancing flashes of steel, I was in the act of resigning my berth on the paper when the chief arrived, and with him a rabble of charmed and enthusiastic friends. Then ensued a scene of riot and carnage such as no human pen, or steel one either, could describe. People were shot, probed, dismembered, blown up, thrown out of the window. There was a brief tornado of murky blasphemy, with a confused and frantic war-dance glimmering through it, and then all was over. In five minutes there was silence, and the gory chief and I sat alone and surveyed the sanguinary ruin that strewed the floor around us.

He said, "You'll like this place when you get used to it."

I said, "I'll have to get you to excuse me; I think maybe I might write to suit you after a while; as soon as I had had some practice and learned the language I am confident I could. But, to speak the plain truth, that sort of energy of expression has its inconveniences, and a man is liable to interruption. You see that yourself. Vigorous writing is calculated to elevate the public, no doubt, but, then I do not like to attract so much attention as it calls forth. I can't write with comfort when I am interrupted so much as I have been to-day. I like this berth well enough, but I don't like to be left here to wait on the customers. The experiences are novel, I grant you, and entertaining too, after a fashion, but they are not judiciously distributed. A gentleman shoots at you through the window and cripples *me*; a bomb-shell comes down the stove-pipe for your gratification and sends the stove-door down *my* throat; a friend drops in to swap compliments with you, and freckles *me* with bullet-holes till my skin won't hold my principles; you go to dinner, and Jones comes with his cowhide, Gillespie throws me out of the window, Thompson tears all my clothes off, and an entire stranger takes my scalp with the easy freedom of an old acquaintance; and in less than five minutes all the blackguards in the country arrive in their war-paint, and proceed to scare the rest of me to death with their tomahawks. Take it altogether, I never had such a spirited time in all my life as I have had to-day. No; I like you, and I like your calm unruffled way of explaining things to the customers, but you see I am not used to it. The Southern heart is too impulsive; Southern hospitality is too lavish with the stranger. The paragraphs which I have written to-day, and into whose cold sentences your masterly hand has infused the fervent spirit of Tennessean journalism, will wake up another nest of hornets. All that mob of editors will come—and they will come hungry, too, and want somebody for breakfast. I shall have to bid you adieu. I decline to be present at these festivities. I came South for my health, I will go back on the same errand, and suddenly. Tennesseean journalism is too stirring for me."

After which we parted with mutual regret, and I took apartments at the hospital.

1869

To Raise Poultry *

SERIOUSLY, from early youth I have taken an especial interest in the subject of poultry-raising, and so this membership touches a ready sympathy in my breast. Even as a school-boy, poultry-raising was a study with me, and I may say without egotism that as early as the age of seventeen I was acquainted with all the best and speediest methods of raising chickens, from raising them off a roost by burning lucifer matches under their noses, down to lifting them off a fence on a frosty night by insinuating the end of a warm board under their heels. By the time I was twenty years old, I really suppose I had raised more poultry than any one individual in all the section round about there. The very chickens came to know my talent, by and by. The youth of both sexes ceased to paw the earth for worms, and old roosters that came to crow, "remained to pray," when I passed by.

I have had so much experience in the raising of fowls that I cannot but think that a few hints from me might be useful to the Society. The two methods I have already touched upon are very simple, and are only used in the raising of the commonest class of fowls; one

* Being a letter written to a Poultry Society that had conferred a complimentary membership upon the author.

is for summer, the other for winter. In the one case you start out with a friend along about eleven o'clock on a summer's night (not later, because in some States—especially in California and Oregon—chickens always rouse up just at midnight and crow from ten to thirty minutes, according to the ease or difficulty they experience in getting the public waked up), and your friend carries with him a sack. Arrived at the hen-roost (your neighbor's, not your own), you light a match and hold it under first one and then another pullet's nose until they are willing to go into that bag without making any trouble about it. You then return home, either taking the bag with you or leaving it behind, according as circumstances shall dictate. *N. B.* I *have* seen the time when it was eligible and appropriate to leave the sack behind and walk off with considerable velocity, without ever leaving any word where to send it.

In the case of the other method mentioned for raising poultry, your friend takes along a covered vessel with a charcoal fire in it, and you carry a long slender plank. This is a frosty night, understand. Arrived at the tree, or fence, or other hen-roost (your own if you are an idiot), you warm the end of your plank in your friend's fire vessel, and then raise it aloft and ease it up gently against a slumbering chicken's foot. If the subject of your attentions is a true bird, he will infallibly return thanks with a sleepy cluck or two, and step out and take up quarters on the plank, thus becoming so conspicuously accessory before the fact to his own murder as to make it a grave question in our minds, as it once was in the mind of Blackstone, whether he is not really and deliberately committing suicide in the second degree.

[But you enter into a contemplation of these legal refinements subsequently—not then].

When you wish to raise a fine, large, donkey-voiced Shanghai rooster, you do it with a lasso, just as you would a bull. It is because he must be choked, and choked effectually, too. It is the only good, certain way, for whenever he mentions a matter which he is cordially interested in, the chances are ninety-nine in a hundred that he secures somebody else's immediate attention to it too, whether it be day or night.

The Black Spanish is an exceedingly fine bird and a costly one. Thirty-five dollars is the usual figure, and fifty a not uncommon price for a specimen. Even its eggs are worth from a dollar to a dollar and a half a-piece, and yet are so unwholesome that the city physician seldom or never orders them for the workhouse. Still I have once or twice procured as high as a dozen at a time for nothing, in the dark of the moon. The best way to raise the Black Spanish fowl is to go late in the evening and raise coop and all. The reason I recommend this method is, that the birds being so valuable, the owners do not permit them to roost around promiscuously, but put them in a coop as strong as a fire-proof safe, and keep it in the kitchen at night. The method I speak of is not always a bright and satisfying success, and yet there are so many little articles of *vertu* about a kitchen, that if you fail on the coop you can generally bring away something else. I brought away a nice steel trap one night, worth ninety cents.

But what is the use in my pouring out my whole intellect on this subject? I have shown the Western New York Poultry Society that they have taken to their bosom a party who is not a spring chicken by any means, but a man who knows all about poultry, and is just as high up in the most efficient methods of raising it as the President of the institution himself. I thank these gentlemen for the honorary membership they have conferred upon me, and shall stand at all times ready and willing to testify my good feeling and my official zeal by deeds as well as by this hastily penned advice and information. Whenever they are ready to go to raising poultry, let them call for me any evening after eleven o'clock, and I shall be on hand promptly.

1869

A Mysterious Visit

THE first notice that was taken of me when I "settled down" recently, was by a gentleman who said he was an assessor, and connected with the U. S. Internal Revenue Department. I said I had never heard of his branch of business before, but I was very glad to see him all the same—would he sit down? He sat down. I did not know anything particular to say, and yet I felt that people who have arrived at the dignity of keeping house must be conversational, must be easy and sociable in company. So, in default of anything else to say, I asked him if he was opening his shop in our neighborhood?

He said he was. [I did not wish to appear ignorant, but I *had* hoped he would mention what he had for sale.]

I ventured to ask him "How was trade?" And he said "So-so."

I then said we would drop in, and if we liked his house as well as any other, we would give him our custom.

He said he thought we would like his establishment well enough to confine ourselves to it—said he never saw anybody who would go off and hunt up another man in his line after trading with him once.

That sounded pretty complacent, but barring that

natural expression of villainy which we all have, the man looked honest enough.

I do not know how it came about exactly, but gradually we appeared to melt down and run together, conversationally speaking, and then everything went along as comfortably as clockwork.

We talked, and talked, and talked—at least I did; and we laughed, and laughed, and laughed—at least he did. But all the time I had my presence of mind about me—I had my native shrewdness turned on "full head," as the engineers say. I was determined to find out all about his business in spite of his obscure answers—and I was determined I would have it out of him without his suspecting what I was at. I meant to trap him with a deep, deep ruse. I would tell him all about my own business, and he would naturally so warm to me during this seductive burst of confidence that he would forget himself, and tell me all about *his* affairs before he suspected what I was about. I thought to myself, My son, you little know what an old fox you are dealing with. I said—

"Now you never would guess what I made lecturing this winter and last spring?"

" No—don't believe I could, to save me. Let me see—let me see. About two thousand dollars, maybe? But no; no, sir, I know you couldn't have made that much. Say seventeen hundred, maybe?"

"Ha! ha! I knew you couldn't. My lecturing receipts for last spring and this winter were fourteen thousand seven hundred and fifty dollars. What do you think of that ?"

"Why, it is amazing—perfectly amazing. I will make

a note of it. And you say even this wasn't all?"

"All! Why bless you, there was my income from the *Daily Warwhoop* for four months—about—about—well, what should you say to about eight thousand dollars, for instance?"

"Say! Why, I should say I should like to see myself rolling in just such another ocean of affluence. Eight thousand! I'll make a note of it. Why man!—and on top of all this I am to understand that you had still more income?"

"Ha! ha! ha! Why, you're only in the suburbs of it, so to speak. There's my book, 'The Innocents Abroad'—price $3.50 to $5.00, according to the binding. Listen to me. Look me in the eye. During the last four months and a half, saying nothing of sales before that, but just simply during the four months and a half, we've sold ninety-five thousand copies of that book. Ninety-five thousand! Think of it. Average four dollars a copy, say. It's nearly four hundred thousand dollars, my son. I get half."

"The suffering Moses! I'll set *that* down. Fourteen-seven-fifty—eight—two hundred. Total, say—well, upon my word, the grand total is about two hundred and thirteen or fourteen thousand dollars! *Is* that possible?"

"Possible! If there's any mistake it's the other way. Two hundred and fourteen thousand, cash, is my income for this year if *I* know how to cipher."

Then the gentleman got up to go. It came over me most uncomfortably that maybe I had made my revelations for nothing, besides being flattered into stretching them considerably by the stranger's astonished exclamations. But no; at the last moment the gentleman handed me a large envelope, and said it contained his advertisement; and that I would find out all about his business in it; and that he would be happy to have my custom—would in fact, be *proud* to have the custom of a man of such prodigious income; and that he used to think there were several wealthy men in the city, but when they came to trade with him, he discovered that they barely had enough to live on; and that, in truth it had been such a weary, weary age since he had seen a rich man face to face, and talked to him, and touched him with his hands, that he could hardly refrain from embracing me—in fact, would esteem it a great favor if I would *let* him embrace me.

This so pleased me that I did not try to resist, but allowed this simple-hearted stranger to throw his arms about me and weep a few tranquilizing tears down the back of my neck. Then he went his way.

As soon as he was gone I opened his advertisement. I studied it attentively for four minutes. I then called up the cook, and said—

"Hold me while I faint! Let Marie turn the griddle-cakes."

By and by, when I came to, I sent down to the rum mill on the corner and hired an artist by the week to sit up nights and curse that stranger, and give me a lift occasionally in the daytime when I came to a hard place.

Ah, what a miscreant he was! His "advertisement" was nothing in the world but a wicked tax-return—a string of impertinent questions about my private affairs, occupying the best part of four foolscap pages of fine print—questions, I may remark, gotten up with such marvelous ingenuity, that the oldest man in the world couldn't understand what the most of them were driving at—questions, too, that were calculated to make a man report about four times his actual income to keep from swearing to a falsehood. I looked for a loophole, but there did not appear to be any. Inquiry No. 1 covered my case as generously and as amply as an umbrella could cover an ant hill—

> "What were your profits, during the past year, from any trade, business, or vocation, wherever carried on?"

And that inquiry was backed up by thirteen others of an equally searching nature, the most modest of which required information as to whether I had committed any burglary or highway robbery, or by any arson or other secret source of emolument, had acquired property which was not enumerated in my statement of income as set opposite to inquiry No.1.

It was plain that that stranger had enabled me to make a goose of myself. It was very, very plain; and so I went out and hired another artist. By working on my vanity, the stranger had seduced me into declaring an income of $214,000. By law, $1000 of this was exempt from income-tax—the only relief I could see, and it was only a drop in the ocean. At the legal five per cent, I must pay to the Government the sum of ten thousand six hundred and fifty dollars, income-tax!

[I may remark, in this place, that I did not do it.]

I am acquainted with a very opulent man, whose house is a palace, whose table is regal, whose outlays are enormous, yet a man who has no income, as I have often noticed by the revenue returns; and to him I went for advice, in my distress. He took my dreadful exhibition of receipts, he put on his glasses, he took his pen, and presto!—I was a pauper! It was the neatest thing that ever was. He did it simply by deftly manipulating the bill of "DEDUCTIONS." He set down my "State, national, and municipal taxes" at so much; my "losses by shipwreck, fire, etc.," at so much; my "losses on sales of real estate"—on "live stock sold"—"on payments for rent of homestead"—on "repairs, improvements, interest"—on "previously taxed salary as an officer of the United States' army, navy, revenue service," and other things. He got astonishing "deductions" out of each and every one of these matters—each and every one of them. And when he was done he handed me the paper, and I saw at a glance that during the year my income, in the way of profits, had been *one thousand two hundred and fifty dollars and forty cents*.

"Now," said he, "the thousand dollars is exempt by law. What you want to do is to go and swear this document in and pay tax on the two hundred and fifty dollars."

[While he was making this speech his little boy Willie lifted a two dollar greenback out of his vest pocket and vanished with it, and I would wager anything that if my stranger were to call on that little boy tomorrow he would make a false return of his income.]

"Do you," said I, "do you always work up the 'deductions' after this fashion in your own case, sir?"

"Well, I should say so! If it weren't for those eleven saving clauses under the head of 'Deduction' I should be beggared every year to support this hateful and wicked, this extortionate and tyrannical government."

This gentleman stands away up among the very best

of the solid men of the city—the men of moral weight, of commercial integrity, of unimpeachable social spotlessness—and so I bowed to his example. I went down to the revenue office, and under the accusing eyes of my old visitor I stood up and swore to lie after lie, fraud after fraud, villainy after villainy, till my soul was coated inches and inches thick with perjury, and myself-respect gone for ever and ever.

But what of it? It is nothing more than thousands of the richest and proudest, and most respected, honored, and courted men in America do every year. And so I don't care. I am not ashamed. I shall simply, for the present, talk little, and eschew fire-proof gloves, lest I fall into certain dreadful habits irrevocably.

1870

A Curious Dream

NIGHT before last I had a singular dream. I seemed to be sitting on a doorstep (in no particular city perhaps), ruminating, and the time of night appeared to be about twelve or one o'clock. The weather was balmy and delicious. There was no human sound in the air, not even a footstep. There was no sound of any kind to emphasize the dead stillness, except the occasional hollow barking of a dog in the distance and the fainter answer of a further dog. Presently up the street I heard a bony clack-clacking, and guessed it was the castanets of a serenading party. In a minute more a tall skeleton, hooded, and half-clad in a tattered and mouldy shroud, whose shreds were flapping about the ribby lattice-work of its person swung by me with a stately stride, and disappeared in the grey gloom of the starlight. It had a broken and worm-eaten coffin on its shoulder and a bundle of something in its hand. I knew what the clack-clacking was then; it was this party's joints working together, and his elbows knocking against his sides as he walked. I may say I was surprised. Before I could collect my thoughts and enter upon any speculations as to what this apparition might portend, I heard another one coming—for I recognized his clack-clack. He had two-thirds of a coffin on his shoulder, and some foot- and head-boards under his arm. I mightily wanted to peer under his hood and speak to him, but when he turned and smiled upon me with his cavernous sockets and his projecting grin as he went by, I thought I would not detain him. He was hardly gone when I heard the clacking again, and another one issued from the shadowy half-light. This one was bending under a heavy gravestone, and dragging a shabby coffin after him by a string. When he got to me he gave me a steady look for a moment or two, and then rounded to and backed up to me, saying:

"Ease this down for a fellow, will you?"

I eased the gravestone down till it rested on the ground, and in doing so noticed that it bore the name of "John Baxter Copmanhurst," with "May, 1839," as the date of his death. Deceased sat wearily down by me, and wiped his os frontis with his major maxillary—chiefly from former habit I judged, for I could not see that he brought away any perspiration.

"It is too bad, too bad," said he, drawing the remnant of the shroud about him and leaning his jaw pensively on his hand. Then he put his left foot up on his knee and fell to scratching his ankle bone absently with a rusty nail which he got out of his coffin.

"What is too bad, friend?"

"Oh, everything, everything. I almost wish I never had died."

"You surprise me. Why do you say this? Has anything gone wrong? What is the matter?"

"Matter! Look at this shroud—rags. Look at this gravestone, all battered up. Look at that disgraceful old coffin. All a man's property going to ruin and destruction before his eyes, and ask him if anything is wrong? Fire and brimstone!"

"Calm yourself, calm yourself," I said. "It *is* too bad—it is certainly too bad, but then I had not supposed that you would much mind such matters, situated as you are."

"Well, my dear sir, I *do* mind them. My pride is hurt, and my comfort is impaired—destroyed, I might say. I will state my case—I will put it to you in such a way that you can comprehend it, if you will let me," said the poor skeleton, tilting the hood of his shroud back, as if he were clearing for action, and thus unconsciously giving himself a jaunty and festive air very much at variance with the grave character of his position in life—so to speak—and in prominent contrast with his distressful mood.

"Proceed," said I.

"I reside in the shameful old graveyard a block or two above you here, in this street—there, now, I just expected that cartilage would let go!—third rib from the bottom, friend, hitch the end of it to my spine with a string, if you have got such a thing about you, though a bit of silver wire is a deal pleasanter, and more durable and becoming, if one keeps it polished—to think of shredding out and going to pieces in this way, just on account of the indifference and neglect of one's posterity!"—and the poor ghost grated his teeth in a way that give me a wrench and a shiver—for the effect is mightily increased by the absence of muffling flesh and cuticle. "I reside in that old graveyard, and have for these thirty years; and I tell you things are changed since I first laid this old tired frame there, and turned over, and stretched out for a long sleep, with a delicious sense upon me of being *done* with bother, and grief, and anxiety, and doubt, and fear, for ever and ever, and listening with comfortable and increasing satisfaction to the sexton's work, from the startling clatter of his first spadeful on my coffin till it dulled away to the faint patting that shaped the roof of my new home—delicious! My! I wish you could try it to-night!" and out of my reverie deceased fetched me with a rattling slap with a bony hand.

"Yes, sir, thirty years ago I laid me down there, and was happy. For it was out in the country, then—out in the breezy, flowery, grand old woods, and the lazy winds gossiped with the leaves, and the squirrels capered over us and around us, and the creeping things visited us, and the birds filled the tranquil solitude with music. Ah, it was worth ten years of a man's life to be dead then! Everything was pleasant. I was in a good neighborhood, for all the dead people that lived near me belonged to the best families in the city. Our posterity appeared to think the world of us. They kept our graves in the very best condition; the fences were always in faultless repair, head-boards were kept painted or whitewashed, and were replaced with new ones as soon as they began to look rusty or decayed; monuments were kept upright, railings intact and bright, the rosebushes and shrubbery trimmed, trained, and free from blemish, the walks clean and smooth and gravelled. But that day is gone by. Our descendants have forgotten us. My grandson lives in a stately house built with money made by these old hands of mine, and I sleep in a neglected grave with invading vermin that gnaw my shroud to build them nests withal! I and friends that lie with me founded and secured the prosperity of this fine city, and the stately bantling of our loves leaves us to rot in a dilapidated cemetery which neighbors curse and strangers scoff at. See the difference between the old time and this—for instance: Our graves are all caved in, now; our head-boards have rotted away and tumbled down; our railings reel this way and that with one foot in the air, after a fashion of unseemly levity; our monuments lean wearily, and our gravestones bow their heads discouraged; there be no adornments any more—no roses, nor shrubs, nor gravelled walks, nor anything that is a comfort to the eye; and even the paintless old board fence that did make a show of holding us sacred from companionship with beasts and the defilement of heedless feet, has tottered till it overhangs the street, and only advertises the presence of our dismal resting-place and invites yet more derision to it. And now we cannot hide our poverty and tatters in the friendly woods, for the city has stretched its withering arms abroad and taken us in, and all that remains of the cheer of our old home is the cluster of lugubrious forest trees that stand, bored and weary of a city life, with their feet in our coffins, looking into the hazy distance and wishing they were there. I tell you it is disgraceful!

"You begin to comprehend—you begin to see how it is. While our descendants are living sumptuously on our money, right around us in the city, we have to fight hard to keep skull and bones together. Bless you, there isn't a grave in our cemetery that doesn't leak—not one. Every time it rains in the night we have to climb out and roost in the trees—and sometimes we are wakened suddenly by the chilly water trickling down the back of our necks. Then I tell you there is a general heaving up of old graves and kicking over of old monuments, and scampering of old skeletons for the trees! Bless me, if you had gone along there some such nights after twelve you might have seen as many as fifteen of us roosting on one limb, with our joints rattling drearily and the wind wheezing through our ribs! Many a time we have perched there for three or four dreary hours, and then come down, stiff and chilled through and drowsy, and borrowed each other's skulls to bale out our graves with—if you will glance up in my mouth, now as I tilt my head back, you can see that my head-piece is half full of old dry sediment—how top-heavy and stupid it makes me sometimes! Yes, sir, many a time if you had happened to come along just before the dawn you'd have caught us baling out the graves and hanging our shrouds on the fence to dry. Why, I had an elegant shroud stolen from there one morning—think a party by the name of Smith took it, that resides in a plebeian graveyard over yonder—I think so because the first time I ever saw him he hadn't anything on but a check-shirt, and the last time I saw him, which was at a social gathering in the new cemetery, he was the best dressed corpse in the company—and it is a significant fact that he left when he saw me; and presently an old woman from here missed her coffin—she generally took it with her when she went anywhere, because she was liable to take cold and bring on the spasmodic rheumatism that originally killed her if she exposed herself to the night air much. She was named Hotchkiss—Anna Matilda

Hotchkiss—you might know her? She has two upper front teeth, is tall, but a good deal inclined to stoop, one rib on the left side gone, has one shred of rusty hair hanging from the left side of her head, and one little tuft just above and a little forward of her right ear, has her under jaw wired on one side where it had worked loose, small bone of left forearm gone—lost in a fight—has a kind of swagger in her gait and a 'gallus' way of going with her arms akimbo and her nostrils in the air—has been pretty free and easy, and is all damaged and battered up till she looks like a queensware crate in ruins—maybe you have met her?"

"God forbid!" I involuntarily ejaculated, for somehow I was not looking for that form of question, and it caught me a little off my guard. But I hastened to make amends for my rudeness, and say, "I simply meant I had not had the honor—for I would not deliberately speak discourteously of a friend of yours. You were saying that you were robbed—and it was a shame, too—but it appears by what is left of the shroud you have on that it was a costly one in its day. How did—"

A most ghastly expression began to develop among the decayed features and shrivelled integuments of my guest's face, and I was beginning to grow uneasy and distressed, when he told me he was only working up a deep, sly smile, with a wink in it, to suggest that about the time he acquired his present garment a ghost in a neighboring cemetery missed one. This reassured me, but I begged him to confine himself to speech thenceforth, because his facial expression was uncertain. Even with the most elaborate care it was liable to miss fire. Smiling should especially be avoided. What *he* might honestly consider a shining success was likely to strike me in a very different light. I said I liked to see a skeleton cheerful, even decorously playful, but I did not think smiling was a skeleton's best hold.

"Yes, friend," said the poor skeleton, "the facts are just as I have given them to you. Two of these old graveyards—the one that I resided in and one further along—have been deliberately neglected by our descendants of to-day until there is no occupying them any longer. Aside from the osteological discomfort of it—and that is no light matter this rainy weather—the present state of things is ruinous to property. We have got to move or be content to see our effects wasted away and utterly destroyed. Now, you will hardly believe it, but it is true, nevertheless, that there isn't a single coffin in good repair among all my acquaintance—now that is an absolute fact. I do not refer to low people who come in a pine box mounted on an express wagon, but I am talking about your high-toned, silver mounted burial-case, your monumental sort, that travel under black plumes at the head of a procession and have choice of cemetery lots—I mean folks like the Jarvises, and the Bledsoes and Burlings, and such. They are all about ruined. The most substantial people in our set, they were. And now look at them—utterly used up and poverty-stricken. One of the Bledsoes actually traded his monument to a late bar-keeper for some fresh shavings to put under his head. I tell you it speaks volumes, for there is nothing a corpse takes so much pride in as his monument. He loves to read the inscription. He comes after awhile to believe what it says himself, and then you may see him sitting on the fence night after night enjoying it. Epitaphs are cheap, and they do a poor chap a world of good after he is dead, especially if he had hard luck while he was alive. I wish they were used more. Now, I don't complain, but confidentially I *do* think it was a little shabby in my descendants to give me nothing but this old slab of a gravestone—and all the more that there isn't a compliment on it. It used to have

'GONE TO HIS JUST REWARD'

on it, and I was proud when I first saw it, but by-and-by I noticed that whenever an old friend of mine came along he would hook his chin on the railing and pull a long face and read along down till he came to that, and then he would chuckle to himself and walk off, looking satisfied and comfortable. So I scratched it off to get rid of those fools. But a dead man always takes a deal of pride in his monument. Yonder goes half-a-dozen of the Jarvises, now, with the family monument along. And Smithers and some hired spectres went by with his a while ago. Hello, Higgins, good-bye, old friend! That's Meredith Higgins—died in '44—belongs to our set in the cemetery—fine old family—great-grandmother was an Injun—I am on the most familiar terms with him—he didn't hear me was the reason he didn't answer me. And I am sorry, too, because I would have liked to introduce you. You would admire him. He is the most disjointed, sway-backed, and generally distorted old skeleton you ever saw, but he is full of fun. When he laughs it sounds like rasping two stones together, and he always starts it off with a cheery screech like raking a nail across a window-pane. Hey, Jones! That is old Columbus Jones—shroud cost four hundred dollars—entire trousseau, including monument, twenty-seven hundred. This was in the Spring of '26. It was enormous style for those days. Dead people came all the way from the Alleghanies to see his things—the party that occupied the grave next to mine remembers it well. Now do you see that individual going along with a piece of a head-board under his arm, one leg-bone below his knee gone, and not a thing in the world on? That is Barstow Dalhousie, and next to Columbus Jones he was the most sumptuously outfitted person that ever entered our cemetery. We are all leaving. We cannot tolerate the treatment we are receiving at the hands of our descendants. They open new cemeteries, but they leave us to our ignominy. They mend the streets, but they never mend anything that is about us or belongs to us. Look at that coffin of mine—yet I tell you in its day it was a piece of furniture that would have attracted attention in any drawing-room in this city. You may have it if you want it—I can't afford to repair it. Put a new bottom in her, and part of a new top, and a bit of fresh lining along the left side, and you'll find her about as comfortable as any receptacle of her species you ever tried. No thanks—no, don't mention it—you have been civil to me, and I would give you all the property I have got before I would seem ungrateful. Now this winding-sheet is a kind of a sweet thing in its way, if you would like to—. No? Well, just as you say, but I wished to be fair and liberal—there's nothing mean about *me*. Good-by, friend, I must be going. I may have a good way to go to-night—don't know. I only know one thing for certain, and that is, that I am on the emigrant trail, now, and I'll never sleep in that crazy old cemetery again. I will travel till I find respectable quarters, if I have to hoof it to New Jersey. All the boys are going. It was decided in public conclave, last night, to emigrate, and by the time the sun rises there won't be a bone left in our old habitations. Such cemeteries may suit my surviving friends, but they do not suit the remains that have the honor to make these remarks. My opinion is the general opinion. If you doubt it, go and see how the departing ghosts upset things before they started. They were almost riotous in their demonstrations of distaste. Hello, here are some of the Bledsoes, and if you will give me a lift with this tombstone I guess I will join company and jog along with them—mighty respectable old family, the Bledsoes, and used to always come out in six-horse hearses, and all that sort of thing fifty years ago when I walked these streets in daylight. Good-by, friend."

And with his gravestone on his shoulder he joined the grisly procession, dragging his damaged coffin after him, for notwithstanding he pressed it upon me so earnestly, I utterly refused his hospitality. I suppose that for as much as two hours these sad outcasts went clacking by, laden with their dismal effects, and all that time I sat pitying them. One or two of the youngest and least dilapidated among them inquired about midnight trains on the railways, but the rest seemed unacquainted with that mode of travel, and merely asked about common public roads to various towns and cities, some of which are not on the map now, and vanished from it and from the earth as much as thirty years ago, and some few of them never *had* existed anywhere but on maps, and private ones in real estate agencies at that. And they asked about the condition of the cemeteries in these towns and cities, and about the reputation the citizens bore as to reverence for the dead.

This whole matter interested me deeply, and likewise compelled my sympathy for these homeless ones. And it all seeming real, and I not knowing it was a dream, I mentioned to one shrouded wanderer an idea that had entered my head to publish an account of this curious and very sorrowful exodus, but said also that I could not describe it truthfully, and just as it occurred, without seeming to trifle with a grave subject and exhibit an irreverence for the dead that would shock and distress their surviving friends. But this bland and stately remnant of a former citizen leaned him far over my gate and whispered in my ear, and said:—

"Do not let that disturb you. The community that can stand such graveyards as those we are emigrating from can stand anything a body can say about the neglected and forsaken dead that lie in them."

At that very moment a cock crowed, and the weird procession vanished and left not a shred or a bone behind. I awoke, and found myself lying with my head out of the bed and "sagging" downwards considerably —a position favorable to dreaming dreams with morals in them, maybe, but not poetry.

NOTE.—The reader is assured that if the cemeteries in his town are kept in good order, this Dream is not levelled at his town at all, but is levelled particularly and venomously at the *next* town.

1870

The Story of the Good Little Boy

ONCE there was a good little boy by the name of Jacob Blivens. He always obeyed his parents, no matter how absurd and unreasonable their demands were; and he always learned his book and never was late at Sabbath-school. He would not play hookey, even when his sober judgment told him it was the most profitable thing he could do. None of the other boys could ever make that boy out, he acted so strangely. He wouldn't lie, no matter how convenient it was. He just said it was wrong to lie, and that was sufficient for him. And he was so honest that he was simply ridiculous. The curious ways that that Jacob had, surpassed everything. He wouldn't play marbles on Sunday, he wouldn't rob birds' nests, he wouldn't give hot pennies to organ-grinders' monkeys; he didn't seem to take any interest in any kind of rational amusement. So the other boys used to try to reason it out and come to an understanding of him, but they couldn't arrive at any satisfactory conclusion. As I said before, they could only figure out a sort of vague idea that he was "afflicted," and so they took him under their protection, and never allowed any harm to come to him.

This good little boy read all the Sunday-school books; they were his greatest delight. This was the whole secret of it. He believed in the good little boys they put in the Sunday-school books; he had every confidence in them. He longed to come across one of them alive, once; but he never did. They all died before his time, maybe. Whenever he read about a particularly good one he turned over quickly to the end to see what became of him, because he wanted to travel thousands of miles and gaze on him; but it wasn't any use; that good little boy always died in the last chapter, and there was a picture of the funeral, with all his relations and the Sunday-school children standing around the grave in pantaloons that were too short, and bonnets that were too large, and everybody crying into handkerchiefs that had as much as a yard and a half of stuff in them. He was always headed off in this way. He never could see one of those good little boys on account of his always dying in the last chapter.

Jacob had a noble ambition to be put in a Sunday-school book. He wanted to be put in, with pictures representing him gloriously declining to lie to his mother, and her weeping for joy about it; and pictures representing him standing on the doorstep giving a penny to a poor beggar-woman with six children, and telling her to spend it freely, but not to be extravagant, because extravagance is a sin; and pictures of him magnanimously refusing to tell on the bad boy who always lay in wait for him around the corner as he came from school, and welted him over the head with a lath, and then chased him home, saying, "Hi! hi!" as he proceeded. That was the ambition of young Jacob Blivens. He wished to be put in a Sunday-school book. It made him feel a little uncomfortable sometimes when he reflected that the good little boys always died. He loved to live, you know, and this was the most unpleasant feature about being a Sunday-school-book boy. He knew it was not healthy to be good. He knew it was more fatal than consumption to be so supernaturally good as the boys in the books were; he knew that none of them had ever been able to stand it long, and it pained him to think that if they put him in a book he wouldn't ever see it, or even if they did get the book out before he died it wouldn't be popular without any picture of his funeral in the back part of it. It couldn't be much of a Sunday-school book that couldn't tell about the advice he gave to the community when he was dying. So at last, of course, he had to make up his mind to do the best he could under the circumstances—to live right, and hang on as long as he could, and have his dying speech all ready when his time came.

But somehow nothing ever went right with this good little boy; nothing ever turned out with him the way it turned out with the good little boys in the books. They always had a good time, and the bad boys had the broken legs; but in his case there was a screw loose somewhere, and it all happened just the other way. When he found Jim Blake stealing apples, and went under the tree to read to him about the bad little boy who fell out of a neighbor's apple-tree and broke his arm, Jim fell out of the tree too, but he fell on *him*, and broke *his* arm, and Jim wasn't hurt at all. Jacob couldn't understand that. There wasn't anything in the books like it.

And once, when some bad boys pushed a blind man

over in the mud, and Jacob ran to help him up and receive his blessing, the blind man did not give him any blessing at all, but whacked him over the head with his stick and said he would like to catch him shoving *him* again, and then pretending to help him up. This was not in accordance with any of the books. Jacob looked them all over to see.

One thing that Jacob wanted to do was to find a lame dog that hadn't any place to stay, and was hungry and persecuted, and bring him home and pet him and have that dog's imperishable gratitude. And at last he found one and was happy; and he brought him home and fed him, but when he was going to pet him the dog flew at him and tore all the clothes off him except those that were in front, and made a spectacle of him that was astonishing. He examined authorities, but he could not understand the matter. It was of the same breed of dogs that was in the books, but it acted very differently. Whatever this boy did he got into trouble. The very things the boys in the books got rewarded for turned out to be about the most unprofitable things he could invest in.

Once, when he was on his way to Sunday-school, he saw some bad boys starting off pleasuring in a sail-boat. He was filled with consternation, because he knew from his reading that boys who went sailing on Sunday invariably got drowned. So he ran out on a raft to warn them, but a log turned with him and slid him into the river. A man got him out pretty soon, and the doctor pumped the water out of him, and gave him a fresh start with his bellows, but he caught cold and lay sick a-bed nine weeks. But the most unaccountable thing about it was that the bad boys in the boat had a good time all day, and then reached home alive and well in the most surprising manner. Jacob Blivens said there was nothing like these things in the books. He was perfectly dumbfounded.

When he got well he was a little discouraged, but he resolved to keep on trying anyhow. He knew that so far his experiences wouldn't do to go in a book, but he hadn't yet reached the allotted term of life for good little boys, and he hoped to be able to make a record yet if he could hold on till his time was fully up. If everything else failed he had his dying speech to fall back on.

He examined his authorities, and found that it was now time for him to go to sea as a cabin-boy. He called on a ship captain and made his application, and when the captain asked for his recommendations he proudly drew out a tract and pointed to the words, "To Jacob Blivens, from his affectionate teacher." But the captain was a coarse, vulgar man, and he said, "Oh, that be blowed! *that* wasn't any proof that he knew how to wash dishes or handle a slush-bucket, and he guessed he didn't want him." This was altogether the most extraordinary thing that ever happened to Jacob in all his life. A compliment from a teacher, on a tract, had never failed to move the tenderest emotions of ship captains, and open the way to all offices of honor and profit in their gift—it never had in any book that ever *he* had read. He could hardly believe his senses.

This boy always had a hard time of it. Nothing ever came out according to the authorities with him. At last, one day, when he was around hunting up bad little boys to admonish, he found a lot of them in the old iron foundry fixing up a little joke on fourteen or fifteen dogs, which they had tied together in long procession, and were going to ornament with empty nitro-glycerine cans made fast to their tails. Jacob's heart was touched. He sat down on one of those cans (for he never minded grease when duty was before him), and he took hold of the foremost dog by the collar, and turned his reproving eye upon wicked Tom Jones. But just at that moment Alderman McWelter, full of wrath, stepped in. All the bad boys ran away, but Jacob Blivens rose in conscious innocence and began one of those stately little Sunday-school-book speeches which always commence with "Oh, sir!" in dead opposition to the fact that no boy, good or bad, ever starts a remark with "Oh, sir." But the alderman never waited to hear the rest. He took Jacob Blivens by the ear and turned him around, and hit him a whack in the rear with the flat of his hand; and in an instant that good little boy shot out through the roof and soared away towards the sun, with the fragments of those fifteen dogs stringing after him like the tail of a kite. And there wasn't a sign of that alderman or that old iron foundry left on the face of the earth; and, as for young Jacob Blivens, he never got a chance to make his last dying speech after all his trouble fixing it up, unless he made it to the birds; because, although the bulk of him came down all right in a tree-top in an adjoining county, the rest of him was apportioned around among four townships, and so they had to hold five inquests on him to find out whether he was dead or not, and how it occurred. You never saw a boy scattered so. *

* This glycerine catastrophe is borrowed from a floating newspaper item, whose author's name I would give if I knew it.—[M. T.]

Thus perished the good little boy who did the best he could, but didn't come out according to the books. Every boy who ever did as he did prospered except him. His case is truly remarkable. It will probably never be accounted for.

1870

How I Edited an Agricultural Paper

I DID not take temporary editorship of an agricultural paper without misgivings. Neither would a landsman take command of a ship without misgivings. But I was in circumstances that made the salary an object. The regular editor of the paper was going off for a holiday, and I accepted the terms he offered, and took his place.

The sensation of being at work again was luxurious, and I wrought all the week with unflagging pleasure. We went to press, and I waited a day with some solicitude to see whether my effort was going to attract any notice. As I left the office, toward sundown, a group of men and boys at the foot of the stairs dispersed with one impulse, and gave me passage-way, and I heard one or two of them say: "That's him!" I was naturally pleased by this incident. The next morning I found a similar group at the foot of the stairs, and scattering couples and individuals standing here and there in the street, and over the way, watching me with interest. The group separated and fell back as I approached, and I heard a man say, "Look at his eye!" I pretended not to observe the notice I was attracting, but secretly I was pleased with it, and was purposing to write an account of it to my aunt. I went up the short flight of stairs, and heard cheery voices and a ringing laugh as I drew near the door, which I opened, and caught a glimpse of two young rural-looking men, whose faces blanched and lengthened when they saw me, and then they both plunged through the window with a great crash. I was surprised.

In about half an hour an old gentleman, with a flowing beard and a fine but rather austere face, entered, and sat down at my invitation. He seemed to have something on his mind. He took off his hat and set it on the floor, and got out of it a red silk handkerchief and a copy of our paper.

He put the paper on his lap, and while he polished his spectacles with his handkerchief, he said, "Are you the new editor?"

I said I was.

"Have you ever edited an agricultural paper before?"

" No," I said; "this is my first attempt."

"Very likely. Have you had any experience in agriculture practically?"

"No; I believe I have not."

"Some instinct told me so," said the old gentleman, putting on his spectacles, and looking over them at me with asperity, while he folded his paper into a convenient shape. "I wish to read you what must have made me have that instinct. It was this editorial. Listen, and see if it was you that wrote it:—

'Turnips should never be pulled, it injures them. It is much better to send a boy up and let him shake the tree."

"Now, what do you think of that?—for I really suppose you wrote it?"

"Think of it? Why, I think it is good. I think it is

sense. I have no doubt that every year millions and millions of bushels of turnips are spoiled in this township alone by being pulled in a half-ripe condition, when, if they had sent a boy up to shake the tree"—

"Shake your grandmother! Turnips don't grow on trees!"

"Oh, they don't, don't they? Well, who said they did? The language was intended to be figurative, wholly figurative. Anybody that knows anything will know that I meant that the boy should shake the vine."

Then this old person got up and tore his paper all into small shreds, and stamped on them, and broke several things with his cane, and said I did not know as much as a cow; and then went out and banged the door after him, and, in short, acted in such a way that I fancied he was displeased about something. But not knowing what the trouble was, I could not be any help to him.

Pretty soon after this a long cadaverous creature, with lanky locks hanging down to his shoulders, and a week's stubble bristling from the hills and valleys of his face, darted within the door, and halted, motionless, with finger on lip, and head and body bent in listening attitude. No sound was heard. Still he listened. No sound. Then he turned the key in the door, and came elaborately tiptoeing toward me till he was within long reaching distance of me, when he stopped, and after scanning my face with intense interest for a while, drew a folded copy of our paper from his bosom, and said—

"There, you wrote that. Read it to me—quick? Relieve me. I suffer."

I read as follows; and as the sentences fell from my

lips I could see the relief come, I could see the drawn muscles relax, and the anxiety go out of the face, and rest and peace steal over the features like the merciful moonlight over a desolate landscape:

"The guano is a fine bird, but great care is necessary in rearing it. It should not be imported earlier than June or later than September. In the winter it should be kept in a warm place, where it can hatch out its young.

"It is evident that we are to have a backward season for grain. Therefore it will be well for the farmer to begin setting out his cornstalks and planting his buckwheat cakes in July instead of August.

"Concerning the pumpkin.—This berry is a favorite with the natives of the interior of New England, who prefer it to the gooseberry for the making of fruit-cake, and who likewise give it the preference over the raspberry for feeding cows, as being more filling and fully as satisfying. The pumpkin is the only esculent of the orange family that will thrive in the North, except the gourd and one or two varieties of the squash. But the custom of planting it in the front yard with the shrubbery is fast going out of vogue, for it is now generally conceded that the pump-kin as a shade tree is a failure.

"Now, as the warm weather approaches, and the ganders begin to spawn"—

The excited listener sprang toward me to shake hands, and said—

"There, there—that will do. I know I am all right now, because you have read it just as I did, word for word. But, stranger, when I first read it this morning, I said to myself, I never, never believed it before, notwithstanding my friends kept me under watch so strict, but now I believe I *am* crazy; and with that I fetched a howl that you might have heard two miles, and started out to kill somebody—because, you know, I knew it would come to that sooner or later, and so I might as well begin. I read one of them paragraphs over again, so as to be certain, and then I burned my house down and started. I have crippled several people, and have got one fellow up a tree, where I can get him if I want him. But I thought I would call in here as I passed along and make the thing perfectly certain; and now it *is* certain, and I tell you it is lucky for the chap that is in the tree. I should have killed him, sure, as I went back. Good-by, sir, good-by; you have taken a great load off my mind. My reason has stood the strain of one of your agricultural articles, and I know that nothing can ever unseat it now. *Good*-by, sir."

I felt a little uncomfortable about the cripplings and arsons this person had been entertaining himself with, for I could not help feeling remotely accessory to them. But these thoughts were quickly banished, for the regular editor walked in! [I thought to myself, Now if you had gone to Egypt as I recommended you to, I might have had a chance to get my hand in; but you wouldn't do it, and here you are. I sort of expected you.]

The editor was looking sad and perplexed and dejected.

He surveyed the wreck which that old rioter and these two young farmers had made, and then said, "This is a sad business—a very sad business. There is the mucilage bottle broken, and six panes of glass, and a spittoon and two candlesticks. But that is not the worst. The reputation of the paper is injured—and permanently, I fear. True, there never was such a call for the paper before, and it never sold such a large edition or soared to such celebrity;—but does one want to be famous for lunacy, and prosper upon the infirmities of his mind? My friend, as I am an honest man, the street out here is full of people, and others are roosting on the fences, waiting to get a glimpse of you, because they think you are crazy. And well they might after reading your editorials. They are a disgrace to journalism. Why, what put it into your head that you could edit a paper of this nature? You do not seem to know the first rudiments of agriculture. You speak of a furrow and a harrow as being the same thing; you talk of the moulting season for cows; and you recommend the domestication of the pole-cat on account of its playfulness and its excellence as a ratter! Your remark that clams will lie quiet if music be played to them was superfluous—entirely superfluous. Nothing disturbs clams. Clams *always* lie quiet. Clams care nothing whatever about music. Ah, heavens and earth, friend! if you had made the acquiring of ignorance the study of your life, you could not have graduated with higher honor than you could to-day. I never saw anything like it. Your observation that the horse-chestnut as an article of commerce is steadily gaining in favor, is simply calculated to destroy this journal. I want you to throw up your situation and go. I want no more holiday—I could not enjoy it if I had it. Certainly not with you in my chair. I would always stand in dread of what you might be going to recommend next. It makes me lose all patience every time I think of your discussing oyster-beds under the head of "Landscape Gardening." I want you to go. Nothing on earth could persuade me to take another holiday. Oh! why didn't you *tell* me you didn't know anything about agriculture?"

"*Tell* you, you cornstalk, you cabbage, you son of a cauliflower? It's the first time I ever heard such an unfeeling remark. I tell you I have been in the editorial business going on fourteen years, and it is the first time I ever heard of a man's having to know anything in order to edit a newspaper. You turnip! Who write the dramatic critiques for the second-rate papers? Why, a parcel of promoted shoemakers and apprentice apothecaries, who know just as much about good acting as I do about good farming and no more. Who review the books? People who never wrote one. Who do up the heavy leaders on finance? Parties who have had the largest opportunities for knowing nothing about it. Who criticize the Indian campaigns? Gentlemen who do not know a war-whoop from a wigwam, and who never have had to run a foot race with a tomahawk, or pluck arrows out of the several members of their families to build the evening camp-fire with. Who write the temperance appeals, and clamor about the flowing bowl? Folks who will never draw another sober breath till they do it in the grave. Who edit the agricultural papers, you—yam? Men, as general thing, who fail in the poetry line, yellow-colored novel line, sensation-drama line, city-editor line, and finally fall back on agriculture as a temporary reprieve from the poor-house. *You* try to tell *me* anything about the newspaper business! Sir, I have been through it from Alpha to Omaha, and I tell you that the less a man knows the bigger the noise he makes and the higher the salary he commands. Heaven knows if I had but been ignorant instead of cultivated, and impudent instead of diffident, I could have made a name for myself in this cold selfish world. I take my leave, sir. Since I have been treated as you have treated me, I am perfectly willing to go. But I have done my duty. I have fulfilled my contract as far as I was permitted to do it. I said I could make your paper of interest to all classes—and I have. I said I could run your circulation up to twenty thousand copies, and if I had had two more weeks I'd have done it. And I'd have given you the best class of readers that ever an agricultural paper had—not a farmer in it, nor a solitary individual who could tell a water-melon tree from a peach-vine to save his life. *You* are the loser by this rupture, not me, Pie-plant. Adios."

I then left.

1870

Political Economy

Political Economy is the basis of all good government. The wisest men of all ages have brought to bear upon this subject the—

[Here I was interrupted and informed that a stranger wished to see me down at the door. I went and confronted him, and asked to know his business, struggling all the time to keep a tight rein on my seething political economy ideas, and not let them break away from me or get tangled in their harness. And privately I wished the stranger was in the bottom of the canal with a cargo of wheat on top of him. I was all in a fever, but he was cool. He said he was sorry to disturb me, but as he was passing he noticed that I needed some lightning-rods. I said, "Yes, yes—go on—what about it?" He said there was nothing about it, in particular—nothing except that he would like to put them up for me. I am new to housekeeping; have been used to hotels and boarding-houses all my life. Like anybody else of similar experience, I try to appear (to strangers) to be an old housekeeper; consequently I said in an off-hand way that I had been intending for some time to have six or eight lightning-rods put up, but— The stranger started, and looked inquiringly at me, but I was serene. I thought that if I chanced to make any mistakes, he would not catch me by my countenance. He said he would rather have my custom than any man's in town. I said, "All right," and started off to wrestle with my great subject again, when he called me back and said it would be necessary to know exactly how many "points" I wanted put up, what parts of the house I wanted them on, and what quality of rod I preferred. It was close quarters for a man not used to the exigencies of housekeeping; but I went through creditably, and he probably never suspected that I was a novice. I told him to put up eight "points," and put them all on the roof, and use the best quality of rod. He said he could furnish the "plain" article at 20 cents a foot; "coppered," 25 cents; "zinc-plated spiral-twist," at 30 cents, that would stop a streak of lightning any time, no matter where it was bound, and "render its errand harmless and its further progress apocryphal." I said apocryphal was no slouch of a word, emanating from the source it did, but, philology aside, I liked the spiral-twist and would take that brand. Then he said he *could* make two hundred and fifty feet answer; but to do it right, and make the best job in town of it, and attract the admiration of the just and the unjust alike, and compel all parties to say they never saw a more symmetrical and hypothetical display of lightning-rods since they were born, he supposed he really couldn't get along without four hundred, though he was not vindictive, and trusted he was willing to try. I said, go ahead and use four hundred, and make any kind of a job he pleased out of it, but let me get back to my work. So I got rid of him at last; and now, after half-an-hour spent in getting my train of political-economy thoughts coupled together again, I am ready to go on once more.]

richest treasures of their genius, their experience of life, and their learning. The great lights of commercial jurisprudence, international confraternity, and biological deviation, of all ages, all civilizations, and all nationalities, from Zoroaster down to Horace Greeley, have—

[Here I was interrupted again, and required to go down and confer further with that lightning-rod man. I hurried off, boiling and surging with prodigious thoughts wombed in words of such majesty that each one of them was in itself a straggling procession of syllables that might be fifteen minutes passing a given point, and once more I confronted him—he so calm and sweet, I so hot and frenzied. He was standing in the contemplative attitude of the Colossus of Rhodes, with one foot on my infant tuberose, and the other among my pansies, his hands on his hips, his hat-brim tilted forward, one eye shut and the other gazing critically and admiringly in the direction of my principal chimney. He said now *there* was a state of things to make a man glad to be alive; and added, "I leave it to *you* if you ever saw anything more deliriously picturesque than eight lightning-rods on one chimney?" I said I had no present recollection of anything that transcended it. He said that in his opinion nothing on earth but Niagara Falls was superior to it in the way of natural scenery. All that was needed now, he verily believed, to make my house a perfect balm to the eye, was to kind of touch up the other chimneys a little, and thus "add to the generous *coup d'œil* a soothing uniformity of achievement which would allay the excitement naturally consequent upon the first *coup d'état*." I asked him if he learned to talk out of a book, and if I could borrow it anywhere? He smiled pleasantly, and said that his manner of speaking was not taught in books, and that nothing but familiarity with lightning could enable a man to handle his conversational style with impunity. He then figured up an estimate, and said that about eight more rods scattered about my roof would about fix me right, and he guessed five hundred feet of stuff would do it; and added that the first eight had got a little the start of him, so to speak, and used up a mere trifle of material more than he had calculated on—a hundred feet or along there. I said I was in a dreadful hurry, and I wished we could get this business permanently mapped out, so that I could go on with my work. He said, "I *could* have put up those eight rods, and marched off about my business—some men *would* have done it. But no: I said to myself, this man is a stranger to me, and I will die before I'll wrong him; there ain't lightning-rods enough on that house, and for one I'll never stir out of my tracks till I've done as I would be done by, and told him so. Stranger, my duty is accomplished; if the recalcitrant and dephlogistic messenger of heaven strikes your"—"There, now, there," I said, "put on the other eight—add five hundred feet of spiral-twist—do anything and everything you want to do; but calm your sufferings, and try to keep your feelings where you can reach them with the dictionary. Meanwhile, if we understand each other now, I will go to work again."

I think I have been sitting here a full hour, this time, trying to get back to where I was when my train of thought was broken up by the last interruption; but I believe I have accomplished it at last, and may venture to proceed again.]

wrestled with this great subject, and the greatest among them have found it a worthy adversary, and one that always comes up fresh and smiling after every throw. The great Confucius said that he would rather be a profound political economist than chief of police. Cicero frequently said that political economy was the grandest consummation that the human mind was capable of consuming; and even our own Greeley has said vaguely but forcibly that "*Political—*

[Here the lightning-rod man sent up another call for me. I went down in a state of mind bordering on impatience. He said he would rather have died than interrupt me, but when he was employed to do a job, and that job was expected to be done in a clean, workmanlike manner, and when it was finished and fatigue urged him to seek the rest and recreation he stood so much in need of, and he was about to do it, but looked up and saw at a glance that all the calculations had been a little out, and if a thunder storm were to come up, and that house, which he felt a personal interest in, stood there with nothing on earth to protect it but sixteen lightning-rods—"Let us have peace!" I shrieked. "Put up a hundred and fifty! Put some on the kitchen! Put a dozen on the barn! Put a couple on the cow!—Put one on the cook!—scatter them all over the persecuted place till it looks like a zinc-plated, spiral-twisted, silver-mounted cane-break! Move! Use up all the material you can get your hands on, and when you run out of lightning-rods put up ram-rods, cam-rods, stair-rods, piston-rods—*anything* that will pander to your dismal appetite for artificial scenery, and bring respite to my raging brain and healing to my lacerated soul!" Wholly unmoved—further than to smile sweetly—this iron being simply turned back his wristbands daintily, and said "He would now proceed to hump himself." Well, all that was nearly three hours ago. It is questionable whether I am calm enough yet to write on the noble theme of political economy, but I cannot resist the desire to try, for it is the one subject that is nearest to my heart and dearest to my brain of all this world's philosophy.]

"*—economy is heaven's best boon to man.*" When the loose but gifted Byron lay in his Venetian exile he observed that, if it could be granted him to go back and live his misspent life over again, he would give his lucid and unintoxicated intervals to the composition, not of frivolous rhymes, but of essays upon political economy. Washington loved this exquisite science; such names as Baker, Beckwith, Judson, Smith, are imperishably linked with it; and even imperial Homer, in the ninth book of the Iliad, has said:—

Fiat justitia, ruat cœlum,
Post mortem unum, ante bellum,
Hic jacet hoc, ex-parte res,
Politicum e-conomico est.

The grandeur of these conceptions of the old poet, together with the felicity of the wording which clothes them, and the sublimity of the imagery whereby they are illustrated, have singled out that stanza, and made it more celebrated than any that ever—

["Now, not a word out of you—not a single word. Just state your bill and relapse into impenetrable silence for ever and ever on these premises. Nine hundred dollars? Is that all? This check for the amount will be honored at any respectable bank in America. What is that multitude of people gathered in the street for? How?— 'looking at the lightning-rods !' Bless my life, did they never see any lightning-rods before? Never saw 'such a stack of them on one establishment,' did I understand you to say? I will step down and critically observe this popular ebullition of ignorance."]

THREE DAYS LATER.—We are all about worn out. For four-and-twenty hours our bristling premises were the talk and wonder of the town. The theatres languished, for their happiest scenic inventions were tame and commonplace compared with my lightning-rods. Our street was blocked night and day with spectators, and among them were many who came from the country to see. It was a blessed relief on the second day, when a thunder storm came up and the lightning began to "go for" my house, as the historian Josephus quaintly phrases it. It cleared the galleries, so to speak. In five minutes there was not a spectator within half a mile of my place; but all the high houses about that distance away were full, windows, roof, and all. And well they might be, for all the falling stars and Fourth-of-July fireworks of a generation, put together and rained down simultaneously out of heaven in one brilliant shower upon one helpless roof, would not have any advantage of the pyrotechnic display that was making my house so magnificently conspicuous in the general gloom of the storm. By actual count, the lightning struck at my establishment seven hundred and sixty-four times in forty minutes, but tripped on one of those faithful rods every time, and slid down the spiral-twist and shot into the earth before it probably had time to be surprised at the way the thing was done. And through all that bombardment only one patch of slates was ripped up, and that was because, for a single instant, the rods in the vicinity were transporting all the lightning they could possibly accommodate. Well, nothing was ever seen like it since the world began. For one whole day and night not a member of my family stuck his head out of the window but he got the hair snatched off it as smooth as a billiard-ball; and if the reader will believe me, not one of us ever dreamt of stirring abroad. But at last the awful siege came to an end—because there was absolutely no more electricity left in the clouds above us within grappling distance of my insatiable rods. Then I sallied forth, and gathered daring workmen together, and not a bite or a nap did we take till the premises were utterly stripped of all their terrific armament except just three rods on the house, one on the kitchen, and one on the barn—and behold these remain there even unto this day. And then, and not till then, the people ventured to use our street again. I will remark here, in passing, that during that fearful time I did not continue my essay upon political economy. I am not even yet settled enough in nerve and brain to resume it.

To Whom It May Concern.—Parties having need of three thousand two hundred and eleven feet of best quality zinc-plated spiral-twist lightning-rod stuff, and sixteen hundred and thirty-one silver-tipped points, all in tolerable repair (and, although much worn by use, still equal to any ordinary emergency), can hear of a bargain by addressing the publisher.

1870

Science vs. Luck

AT that time, in Kentucky (said the Hon. Mr. K—), the law was very strict against what is termed "games of chance." About a dozen of the boys were detected playing "seven-up" or "old sledge" for money, and the grand jury found a true bill against them. Jim Sturgis was retained to defend them when the case came up, of course. The more he studied over the matter, and looked into the evidence, the plainer it was that he must lose a case at last—there was no getting around that painful fact. Those boys had certainly been betting money on a game of chance. Even public sympathy was roused in behalf of Sturgis. People said it was a pity to see him mar his successful career with a big prominent case like this, which must go against him.

But after several restless nights an inspired idea flashed upon Sturgis, and he sprang out of bed delighted. He thought he saw his way through. The next day he whispered around a little among his clients and a few friends, and then when the case came up in court he acknowledged the seven-up and the betting, and, as his sole defence, had the astounding effrontery to put in the plea that old sledge was not a game of chance! There was the broadest sort of a smile all over the faces of that sophisticated audience. The judge smiled with the rest. But Sturgis maintained a countenance whose earnestness was even severe. The opposite counsel tried to ridicule him out of his position, and did not succeed. The judge jested in a ponderous judicial way about the thing, but did not move him. The matter was becoming grave. The judge lost a little of his patience, and said the joke had gone far enough. Jim Sturgis said he knew of no joke in the matter—his clients could not be punished for indulging in what some people chose to consider a game of chance until it was *proven* that it was a game of chance. Judge and counsel said that would be an easy matter, and forthwith called Deacons Job, Peters, Burke, and Johnson, and Dominies Wirt and Miggles, to testify; and they unanimously and with strong feeling put down the legal quibble of Sturgis by pronouncing that old sledge *was* a game of chance.

"What do you call it *now*?" said the judge.

"I call it a game of science!" retorted Sturgis; "and I'll prove it, too !"

They saw his little game.

He brought in a cloud of witnesses, and produced an overwhelming mass of testimony, to show that old sledge was not a game of chance but a game of science.

Instead of being the simplest case in the world, it had somehow turned out to be an excessively knotty one. The judge scratched his head over it a while, and said there was no way of coming to a determination, because just as many men could be brought into court who would testify on one side as could be found to testify on the other. But he said he was willing to do the fair thing by all parties, and would act upon any suggestion Mr.

Sturgis would make for the solution of the difficulty.

Mr. Sturgis was on his feet in a second.

"Impanel a jury of six of each, Luck *versus* Science. Give them candles and a couple of decks of cards. Send them into the jury room, and just abide by the result!"

There was no disputing the fairness of the proposition. The four deacons and the two dominies were sworn in as the "chance" jurymen, and six inveterate old seven-up professors were chosen to represent the "science" side of the issue. They retired to the jury room.

In about two hours Deacon Peters sent into court to borrow three dollars from a friend. [Sensation.] In about two hours more Dominie Miggles sent into court to borrow a "stake" from a friend. [Sensation.] During the next three or four hours the other dominie and the other deacons sent into court for small loans. And still the packed audience waited, for it was a prodigious occasion in Bull's Corners, and one in which every father of a family was necessarily interested.

The rest of the story can be told briefly. About daylight the jury came in, and Deacon Job, the foreman, read the following

VERDICT.

We, the jury in the case of the Commonwealth of Kentucky vs. John Wheeler *et al.*, have carefully considered the points of the case, and tested the merits of the several theories advanced, and do hereby unanimously decide that the game commonly known as old sledge or seven-up is eminently a game of science and not of chance. In demonstration whereof it is hereby and herein stated, iterated, reiterated, set forth, and made manifest that, during the entire night, the "chance" men never won a game or turned a jack, although both feats were common and frequent to the opposition; and furthermore, in support of this our verdict, we call attention to the significant fact that the "chance" men are all busted, and the "science" men have got the money. It is the deliberate opinion of this jury, that the "chance" theory concerning seven-up is a pernicious doctrine, and calculated to inflict untold suffering and pecuniary loss upon any community that takes stock in it.

"That is the way that seven-up came to be set apart and particularized in the statute-books of Kentucky as being a game not of chance but of science, and therefore not punishable under the law," said Mr. K—. "That verdict is of record, and holds good to this day."

1870

My Watch

AN INSTRUCTIVE LITTLE TALE

MY beautiful new watch had run eighteen months without losing or gaining, and without breaking any part of its machinery or stopping. I had come to believe it infallible in its judgments about the time of day, and to consider its constitution and its anatomy imperishable. But at last, one night, I let it run down. I grieved about it as if it were a recognized messenger and forerunner of calamity. But by-and-by I cheered up, set the watch by guess, and commanded my bodings and superstitions to depart. Next day I stepped into the chief jeweler's to set it by the exact time, and the head of the establishment took it out of my hand and proceeded to set it for me. Then he said, "She is four minutes slow—regulator wants pushing up." I tried to stop him—tried to make him understand that the watch kept perfect time. But no; all this human cabbage could see was that the watch was four minutes slow, and the regulator *must* be pushed up a little; and so, while I danced around him in anguish, and implored him to let the watch alone, he calmly and cruelly did the shameful deed. My watch began to gain. It gained faster and faster day by day. Within the week it sickened to a raging fever, and its pulse went up to a hundred and fifty in the shade. At the end of two months it had left all the timepieces of the town far in the rear, and was a fraction over thirteen days ahead of the almanac. It was away into November enjoying the snow, while the October leaves were still turning. It hurried up house rent, bills payable, and such things, in such a ruinous way that I could not abide it. I took it to the watchmaker to be regulated. He asked me if I had ever had it repaired. I said no, it had never needed any repairing. He looked a look of vicious happiness and eagerly pried the watch open, and then put a small dice box into his eye and peered into its machinery. He said it wanted cleaning and oiling, besides regulating—come in a week. After being cleaned and oiled, and regulated, my watch slowed down to that degree that it ticked like a tolling bell. I began to be left by trains, I failed all appointments, I got to missing my dinner; my watch strung out three days' grace to four and let me go to protest; I gradually drifted back into yesterday, then day before, then into last week, and by-and-by the comprehension came upon me that all solitary and alone I was lingering along in week before last, and the world was out of sight. I seemed to detect in myself a sort of sneaking fellow-feeling for the mummy in the museum, and a desire to swap news with him. I went to a watchmaker again. He took the watch all to pieces while I waited, and then said the barrel was "swelled." He said he could reduce it in three days. After this the watch *averaged* well, but nothing more. For half a day it would go like the very mischief, and keep up such a barking and wheezing, and whooping and sneezing and snorting, that I could not hear myself think for the disturbance; and as long as it held out there was not a watch in the land that stood any chance against it. But the rest of the day it would keep on slowing down and fooling along until all the clocks it had left behind caught up again. So at last, at the end of twenty-four hours, it would trot up to the judges' stand all right and just in time. It would show a fair and square average, and no man could say it had done more or less than its duty. But a correct average is only a mild virtue in a watch, and I took this instrument to another watchmaker. He said the kingbolt was broken. I said I was glad it was nothing more serious. To tell the plain truth, I had no idea what the kingbolt was, but I did not choose to appear ignorant to a stranger. He repaired the kingbolt, but what the watch gained in one way it lost in another. It would run awhile and then stop awhile, and then run awhile again, and so on, using its own discretion about the intervals. And every time it went off it kicked back like a musket. I padded my breast for a few days, but finally took the watch to another watchmaker. He picked it all to pieces, and turned the ruin over and over under his glass; and then he said there appeared to be something the matter with the hair-trigger. He fixed it, and gave it a fresh start. It did well now, except that always at ten minutes to ten the hands would shut together like a pair of scissors, and from that time forth they would travel together. The oldest man in the world could not make head or tail of the time of day by such a watch, and so I went again to have the thing repaired. This person said that the crystal had got bent, and that the mainspring was not straight. He also remarked that part of the works needed half-soling. He made these things all right, and then my timepiece performed unexceptionably, save that now and then, after working along quietly for nearly eight hours, everything inside would let go all of a sudden and begin to buzz like a bee, and the hands would straightway begin to spin round and round so fast that their individuality was lost completely, and they simply seemed a delicate spider's web over the face of the watch. She would reel off the next twenty-four hours in six or seven minutes, and then stop with a bang. I went with a heavy heart to one more watchmaker, and looked on while he took her to pieces. Then I prepared to cross-question him rigidly, for this thing was getting serious. The watch had cost two hundred dollars originally, and I seemed to have paid out two or three thousand for repairs. While I waited and looked on I presently recognized in this watchmaker an old acquaintance—a steamboat engineer of other days, and not a good engineer either. He examined all the parts carefully, just as the other watchmakers had done, and then delivered his verdict with the same confidence of manner.

He said—

"She makes too much steam—you want to hang the monkey-wrench on the safety-valve!"

I brained him on the spot, and had him buried at my own expense.

My uncle William (now deceased, alas!) used to say that a good horse was a good horse until it had run away once, and that a good watch was a good watch until the repairers got a chance at it. And he used to wonder what became of all the unsuccessful tinkers, and gunsmiths, and shoemakers, and engineers, and blacksmiths; but nobody could ever tell him.

1870

Running For Governor

A FEW months ago I was nominated for Governor of the great State of New York, to run against Mr. John T. Smith and Mr. Blank J. Blank on an independent ticket. I somehow felt that I had one prominent advantage over these gentlemen, and that was—good character. It was easy to see by the newspapers that if ever they had known what it was to bear a good name, that time had gone by. It was plain that in these latter years they had become familiar with all manner of shameful crimes. But at the very moment that I was exalting my advantage and joying in it in secret, there was a muddy undercurrent of discomfort "riling" the deeps of my happiness, and that was—the having to hear my name bandied about in familiar connection with those of such people. I grew more and more disturbed. Finally I wrote my grandmother about it. Her answer came quick and sharp. She said—

"You have never done one single thing in all your life to be ashamed of—not one. Look at the newspapers—look at them and comprehend what sort of characters Messrs. Smith and Blank are, and then see if you are willing to lower yourself to their level and enter a public canvass with them."

It was my very thought! I did not sleep a single moment that night. But after all I could not recede. I was fully committed, and must go on with the fight. As I was looking listlessly over the papers at breakfast I came across this paragraph, and I may truly say I never was so confounded before.

"PERJURY.—Perhaps, now that Mr. Mark Twain is before the people as a candidate for Governor, he will condescend to explain how he came to be convicted of perjury by thirty-four witnesses in Wakawak, Cochin China, in 1863, the intent of which perjury being to rob a poor native widow and her helpless family of a meagre plantain-patch, their only stay and support in their bereavement and desolation. Mr. Twain owes it to himself, as well as to the great people whose suffrages he asks, to clear this matter up. Will he do it?"

I thought I should burst with amazement! Such a cruel, heartless charge. I never had *seen* Cochin China! I never had *heard* of Wakawak! I didn't know a plantain-patch from a kangaroo! I did not know what to do. I was crazed and helpless. I let the day slip away without doing anything at all. The next morning the same paper had this—nothing more:—

"SIGNIFICANT.—Mr. Twain, it will be observed, is suggestively silent about the Cochin China perjury."

[*Mem.*—During the rest of the campaign this paper never referred to me in any other way than as "the infamous perjurer Twain."]

Next came the *Gazette*, with this:—

"WANTED TO KNOW.—Will the new candidate for Governor deign to explain to certain of his fellow-citizens (who are suffering to vote for him!) the little circumstance of his cabin-mates in Montana losing small valuables from time to time, until at last, these things having been invariably found on Mr. Twain's person or in his 'trunk' (newspaper he rolled his traps in), they felt compelled to give him a friendly admonition for his own good, and so tarred and feathered him, and rode him on a rail, and then advised him to leave a permanent vacuum in the place he usually occupied in the camp. Will he do this?"

Could anything be more deliberately malicious than that? For I never was in Montana in my life.

[After this, this journal customarily spoke of me as "Twain, the Montana Thief."]

I got to picking up papers apprehensively—much as one would lift a desired blanket which he had some idea might have a rattlesnake under it. One day this met my eye:—

"THE LIE NAILED!—By the sworn affidavits of Michael O'Flanagan, Esq., of the Five Points, and Mr. Snub Rafferty and Mr. Catty Mulligan, of Water Street, it is established that Mr. Mark Twain's vile statement that the lamented grandfather of our noble standard bearer, Blank J. Blank, was hanged for highway robbery, is a brutal and gratuitous LIE, without a shadow of foundation in fact. It is disheartening to virtuous men to see such shameful means resorted to to achieve political success as the attacking of the dead in their graves, and defiling their honored names with slander. When we think of the anguish this miserable falsehood must cause the innocent relatives and friends of the deceased, we are almost driven to incite an outraged and insulted public to summary and unlawful vengeance upon the traducer. But no! let us leave him to the agony of a lacerated conscience (though if passion should get the better of the public, and in its blind fury they should do the traducer bodily injury, it is but too obvious that no jury could convict and no court punish the perpetrators of the deed)."

The ingenious closing sentence had the effect of moving me out of bed with despatch that night, and out at the back door also, while the "outraged and insulted public" surged in the front way, breaking furniture and windows in their righteous indignation as they came, and taking off such property as they could carry when they went. And yet I can lay my hand upon the Book and say that I never slandered Mr. Blank's grandfather. More: I had never even heard of him or mentioned him up to that day and date.

[I will state, in passing, that the journal above quoted from always referred to me afterward as "Twain, the Body-Snatcher."]

The next newspaper article that attracted my attention was the following:—

> "A SWEET CANDIDATE.—Mr. Mark Twain, who was to make such a blighting speech at the mass meeting of the Independents last night, didn't come to time! A telegram from his physician stated that he had been knocked down by a runaway team, and his leg broken in two places—sufferer lying in great agony, and so forth and so forth, and a lot more bosh of the same sort And the Independents tried hard to swallow the wretched subterfuge, and pretend that they did not know what was the *real* reason of the absence of the abandoned creature whom they denominate their standard-bearer. *A certain man was seen to reel into Mr. Twain's hotel last night in a state of beastly intoxication*. It is the imperative duty of the Independents to prove that this besotted brute was not Mark Twain himself. We have them at last! This is a case that admits of no shirking. The voice of the people demands in thunder-tones 'WHO WAS THAT MAN?' "

It was incredible, absolutely incredible, for a moment, that it was really my name that was coupled with this disgraceful suspicion. Three long years had passed over my head since I had tasted ale, beer, wine, or liquor of any kind.

[It shows what effect the times were having on me when I say that I saw myself confidently dubbed "Mr. Delirium Tremens Twain" in the next issue of that journal without a pang—notwithstanding I knew that with monotonous fidelity the paper would go on calling me so to the very end.]

By this time anonymous letters were getting to be an important part of my mail matter. This form was common—

"How about that old woman you kiked of your premisers which was beging. POL PRY."

And this—

"There is things which you have done which is unbeknowens to anybody but me. You better trot out a few dols. to yours truly, or you'll hear thro' the papers from HANDY ANDY."

This is about the idea. I could continue them till the reader was surfeited, if desirable.

Shortly the principal Republican journal "convicted" me of wholesale bribery, and the leading Democratic paper "nailed" an aggravated case of blackmailing to me.

[In this way I acquired two additional names: "Twain the Filthy Corruptionist," and "Twain the Loathsome Embracer."]

By this time there had grown to be such a clamor for an "answer" to all the dreadful charges that were laid to me that the editors and leaders of my party said it would be political ruin for me to remain silent any longer. As if to make their appeal the more imperative, the following appeared in one of the papers the very next day:—

"BEHOLD THE MAN!—The independent candidate still maintains silence. Because he dare not speak. Every accusation against him has been amply proved, and they have been endorsed and re-endorsed by his own eloquent silence, till at this day he stands for ever convicted. Look upon your candidate, Independents! Look upon the Infamous Perjurer! the Montana Thief! the Body-Snatcher! Contemplate your incarnate Delirium Tremens! your Filthy Corruptionist! your Loathsome Embracer! Gaze upon him—ponder him well—and then say if you can give your honest votes to a creature who has earned this dismal array of titles by his hideous crimes, and dares not open his mouth in denial of any one of them!"

There was no possible way of getting out of it, and so in deep humiliation, I set about preparing to "answer" a mass of baseless charges and mean and wicked falsehoods. But I never finished the task, for the very next morning a paper came out with a new horror, a fresh malignity, and seriously charged me with burning a lunatic asylum with all its inmates, because it obstructed the view from my house. This threw me into a sort of panic. Then came the charge of poisoning my uncle to get his property, with an imperative demand that the grave should be opened. This drove me to the verge of distraction. On top of this I was accused of employing toothless and incompetent old relatives to prepare the food for the foundling hospital when I was warden. I was wavering—wavering. And at last, as a due and fitting climax to the shameless persecution that party rancor had inflicted upon me, nine little toddling children, of all shades of color and degrees of raggedness, were taught to rush on to the platform at a public meeting, and clasp me around the legs and call me PA!

I gave it up. I hauled down my colors and surrendered. I was not equal to the requirements of a Gubernatorial campaign in the State of New York, and so I sent in my withdrawal from the candidacy, and in bitterness of spirit signed it, "Truly yours, *once* a decent man, but now

MARK TWAIN, I. P., M. T., B. S., D. T., F. C., and L. E."

1870

History Repeats Itself

THE following I find in a Sandwich Island paper which some friend has sent me from that tranquil far-off retreat. The coincidence between my own experience and that here set down by the late Mr. Benton is so remarkable that I cannot forbear publishing and commenting upon the paragraph. The Sandwich Island paper says:—

> "How touching is this tribute of the late Hon. T. H. Benton to his mother's influence:—'My mother asked me never to use tobacco; I have never touched it from that time to the present day. She asked me not to gamble, and I have never gambled. I cannot tell who is losing in games that are being played. She admonished me, too, against liquor-drinking, and whatever capacity for endurence I have at present, and whatever usefulness I may have attained through life, I attribute to having complied with her pious and correct wishes. When I was seven years of age she asked me not to drink, and then I made a resolution of total abstinence; and that I have adhered to it through all time I owe to my mother.' "

I never saw anything so curious. It is almost an exact epitome of my own moral career—after simply substituting a grandmother for a mother. How well I remember my grandmother's asking me not to use tobacco, good old soul! She said, "You're at it again, are you, you whelp? Now, don't ever let me catch you chewing tobacco before breakfast again, or I lay I'll blacksnake you within an inch of your life!" I have never touched it at that hour of the morning from that time to the present day.

She asked me not to gamble. She whispered and said, "Put up those wicked cards this minute!—two pair and a jack, you numskull, and the other fellow's got a flush!"

I never have gambled from that day to this—never once—without a "cold deck" in my pocket. I cannot even tell who is going to lose in games that are being played unless I dealt myself.

When I was two years of age she asked me not to drink, and then I made a resolution of total abstinence. That I have adhered to it and enjoyed the beneficent effects of it through all time, I owe to my grandmother. I have never drunk a drop from that day to this of any kind of water.

1870

My First Literary Venture

I WAS a very smart child at the age of thirteen—an unusually smart child, I thought at the time. It was then that I did my first newspaper scribbling, and most unexpectedly to me it stirred up a fine sensation in the community. It did, indeed, and I was very proud of it, too. I was a printer's "devil," and a progressive and aspiring one. My uncle had me on his paper (the *Weekly Hannibal Journal*, two dollars a year in advance—five hundred subscribers, and they paid in cordwood, cabbages, and unmarketable turnips), and on a lucky summer's day he left town to be gone a week, and asked me if I thought I could edit one issue of the paper judiciously. Ah! didn't I want to try! Higgins was the editor on the rival paper. He had lately been jilted, and one night a friend found an open note on the poor fellow's bed, in which he stated that he could no longer endure life and had drowned himself in Bear Creek. The friend ran down there and discovered Higgins wading back to shore! He had concluded he wouldn't. The village was full of it for several days, but Higgins did not suspect it. I thought this was a fine opportunity. I wrote an elaborately wretched account of the whole matter, and then illustrated it with villainous cuts engraved on the bottoms of wooden type with a jack-knife—one of them a picture of Higgins wading out into the creek in his shirt, with a lantern, sounding the depth of the water with a walking-stick. I thought it was desperately funny, and was densely unconscious that there was any moral obliquity about such a publication. Being satisfied with this effort I looked around for other worlds to conquer, and it struck me that it would make good, interesting matter to charge the editor of a neighboring country paper with a piece of gratuitous rascality and "see him squirm."

I did it, putting the article into the form of a parody on the Burial of "Sir John Moore"—and a pretty crude parody it was, too.

Then I lampooned two prominent citizens outrageously—not because they had done anything to deserve it, but merely because I thought it was my duty to make the paper lively.

Next I gently touched up the newest stranger—the lion of the day, the gorgeous journeyman tailor from Quincy. He was a simpering coxcomb of the first water, and the "loudest" dressed man in the State. He was an inveterate woman-killer. Every week he wrote lushy "poetry" for the "Journal," about his newest conquest. His rhymes for my week were headed, "To Mary in H—l," meaning to Mary in Hannibal, of course. But while setting up the piece I was suddenly riven from head to heel by what I regarded as a perfect thunderbolt of humor, and I compressed it into a snappy foot-note at the bottom—thus:—"We will let this thing pass, just this once; but we wish Mr. J. Gordon Runnels to understand distinctly that we have a character to sustain, and from this time forth when he wants to commune with his friends in h—l, he must select some other medium than the columns of this journal!"

The paper came out, and I never knew any little thing attract so much attention as those playful trifles of mine.

For once the *Hannibal Journal* was in demand—a novelty it had not experienced before. The whole town was stirred. Higgins dropped in with a double-barrelled shot-gun early in the forenoon. When he found that it was an infant (as he called me) that had done him the damage, he simply pulled my ears and went away; but he threw up his situation that night and left town for good. The tailor came with his goose and a pair of shears; but he despised me too, and departed for the South that night. The two lampooned citizens came with threats of libel, and went away incensed at my insignificance. The country editor pranced in with a warwhoop next day, suffering for blood to drink; but he ended by forgiving me cordially and inviting me down to the drug store to wash away all animosity in a friendly bumper of "Fahnestock's Vermifuge." It was his little joke. My uncle was very angry when he got back—unreasonably so, I thought, considering what an impetus I had given the paper, and considering also that gratitude for his preservation ought to have been uppermost in his mind, inasmuch as by his delay he had so wonderfully escaped dissection, tomahawking, libel, and getting his head shot off. But he softened when he looked at the accounts and saw that I had actually booked the unparalleled number of thirty-three new subscribers, and had the vegetables to show for it, cordwood, cabbage, beans, and unsalable turnips enough to run the family for two years!

1871

About Barbers

ALL things change except barbers, the ways of barbers, and the surroundings of barbers. These never change. What one experiences in a barber's shop the first time he enters one is what he always experiences in barbers' shops afterwards till the end of his days. I got shaved this morning as usual. A man approached the door from Jones Street as I approached it from Main—a thing that always happens. I hurried up, but it was of no use; he entered the door one little step ahead of me, and I followed in on his heels and saw him take the only vacant chair, the one presided over by the best barber. It always happens so. I sat down, hoping that I might fall heir to the chair belonging to the better of the remaining two barbers, for he had already begun combing his man's hair, while his comrade was not yet quite done rubbing up and oiling his customer's locks. I watched the probabilities with strong interest. When I saw that No.2 was gaining on No.1 my interest grew to solicitude. When No. 1 stopped a moment to make change on a bath ticket for a new comer, and lost ground in the race, my solicitude rose to anxiety. When No.1 caught up again, and both he and his comrade were pulling the towels away and brushing the powder from their customers' cheeks, and it was about an even thing which one would say "Next!" first, my very breath stood still with the suspense. But when at the culminating moment No.1 stopped to pass a comb a couple of times through his customer's eyebrows, I saw that he had lost the race by a single instant, and I rose indignant and quitted the shop, to keep from falling into the hands of No.2; for I have none of that enviable firmness that enables a man to look calmly into the eyes of a waiting barber and tell him he will wait for his fellow-barber's chair.

I stayed out fifteen minutes, and then went back, hoping for better luck. Of course all the chairs were occupied now, and four men sat waiting, silent, unsociable, distraught, and looking bored, as men always do who are awaiting their turn in a barber's shop. I sat down in one of the iron-armed compartments of an old sofa, and put in the time for a while reading the framed advertisements of all sorts of quack nostrums for dyeing and coloring the hair. Then I read the greasy names on the private bay rum bottles; read the names and noted the numbers on the private shaving cups in the pigeon-holes; studied the stained and damaged cheap prints on the walls, of battles, early Presidents, and voluptuous recumbent sultanas, and the tiresome and everlasting young girl putting her grandfather's spectacles on; execrated in my heart the cheerful canary and the distracting parrot that few barbers' shops are without. Finally, I searched out the least dilapidated of last year's illustrated papers that littered the foul centre-table, and conned their unjustifiable misrepresentations of old forgotten events.

At last my turn came. A voice said "Next!" and I

surrendered to—No.2, of course. It always happens so. I said meekly that I was in a hurry, and it affected him as strongly as if he had never heard it. He shoved up my head, and put a napkin under it. He ploughed his fingers into my collar and fixed a towel there. He explored my hair with his claws and suggested that it needed trimming. I said I did not want it trimmed. He explored again and said it was pretty long for the present style—better have a little taken off; it needed it behind especially. I said I had had it cut only a week before. He yearned over it reflectively a moment, and then asked with a disparaging manner, who cut it? I came back at him promptly with a "You did!" I had him there. Then he fell to stirring up his lather and regarding himself in the glass, stopping now and then to get close and examine his chin critically or inspect a pimple. Then he lathered one side of my face thoroughly, and was about to lather the other, when a dog fight attracted his attention, and he ran to the window and stayed and saw it out, losing two shillings on the result in bets with the other barbers, a thing which gave me great satisfaction. He finished lathering, and then began to rub in the suds with his hand. He now began to sharpen his razor on an old suspender, and was delayed a good deal on account of a controversy about a cheap masquerade ball he had figured at the night before, in red cambric and bogus ermine, as some kind of a king. He was so gratified with being chaffed about some damsel whom he had smitten with his charms that he used every means to continue the controversy by pretending to be annoyed at the chaffings of his fellows. This matter begot more surveyings of himself in the glass, and he put down his razor and brushed his hair with elaborate care, plastering an inverted arch of it down on his forehead, accomplishing an accurate "part" behind, and brushing the two wings forward over his ears with nice exactness. In the meantime the lather was drying on my face, and apparently eating into my vitals.

Now he began to shave, digging his fingers into my countenance to stretch the skin and bundling and tumbling my head this way and that as convenience in shaving demanded. As long as he was on the tough sides of my face I did not suffer; but when he began to rake, and rip, and tug at my chin, the tears came. He now made a handle of my nose, to assist him in shaving the corners of my upper lip, and it was by this bit of circumstantial evidence that I discovered that a part of his duties in the shop was to clean the kerosene lamps. I had often wondered in an indolent way whether the barbers did that, or whether it was the boss. About this time I was amusing myself trying to guess where he would be most likely to cut me this time, but he got ahead of me, and sliced me on the end of the chin before I had got my mind made up. He immediately sharpened his razor—he might have done it before. I do not like a close shave, and would not let him go over me a second time. I tried to get him to put up his razor, dreading that he would make for the side of my chin, my pet tender spot, a place which a razor cannot touch twice without making trouble; but he said he only wanted to just smooth off one little roughness, and in the same moment he slipped his razor along the forbidden ground, and the dreaded pimple-signs of a close shave rose up smarting and answered to the call. Now he soaked his towel in bay rum, and slapped it all over my face nastily; slapped it over as if a human being ever yet washed his face in that way. Then he dried it by slapping with the dry part of the towel; as if a human being ever dried his face in such a fashion; but a barber seldom rubs you like a Christian. Next he poked bay rum into the cut place with his towel, then choked the wound with powdered starch, then soaked it with bay rum again, and would have gone on soaking and powdering it for evermore, no doubt, if I had not rebelled and begged off. He powdered my whole face now, straightened me up, and began to plough my hair thoughtfully with his hands. Then he suggested a shampoo, and said my hair needed it badly, very badly. I observed that I shampooed it myself very thoroughly in the bath yesterday. I "had him" again. He next recommended some of "Smith's Hair Glorifier," and offered to sell me a bottle. I declined. He praised the new perfume, "Jones' Delight of the Toilet," and proposed to sell me some of that. I declined again. He tendered me a tooth-wash atrocity of his own invention, and when I declined offered to trade knives with me.

He returned to business after the miscarriage of this last enterprise, sprinkled me all over, legs and all, greased my hair in defiance of my protest against it, rubbed and scrubbed a good deal of it out by the roots, and combed and brushed the rest, parting it behind, and plastering the eternal inverted arch of hair down on my forehead, and then, while combing my scant eyebrows and defiling them with pomade, strung out an account of the achievements of a six-ounce black and tan terrier of his till I heard the whistles blow for noon, and knew I was five minutes too late for the train. Then he snatched away the towel, brushed it lightly about my face, passed his comb through my eyebrows once more, and gaily sang out "Next!"

This barber fell down and died of apoplexy two hours later. I am waiting over a day for my revenge—I am going to attend his funeral.

1871

Buck Fanshaw's Funeral

SOMEBODY has said that in order to know a community, one must observe the style of its funerals and know what manner of men they bury with most ceremony. I cannot say which class we buried with most eclat in our "flush times," the distinguished public benefactor or the distinguished rough—possibly the two chief grades or grand divisions of society honored their illustrious dead about equally; and hence, no doubt the philosopher I have quoted from would have needed to see two representative funerals in Virginia before forming his estimate of the people.

There was a grand time over Buck Fanshaw when he died. He was a representative citizen. He had "killed his man"—not in his own quarrel, it is true, but in defence of a stranger unfairly beset by numbers. He had kept a sumptuous saloon. He had been the proprietor of a dashing helpmeet whom he could have discarded without the formality of a divorce. He had held a high position in the fire department and been a very Warwick in politics. When he died there was great lamentation throughout the town, but especially in the vast bottom-stratum of society.

On the inquest it was shown that Buck Fanshaw, in the delirium of a wasting typhoid fever, had taken arsenic, shot himself through the body, cut his throat, and jumped out of a four-story window and broken his neck—and after due deliberation, the jury, sad and tearful, but with intelligence unblinded by its sorrow, brought in a verdict of death "by the visitation of God." What could the world do without juries?

Prodigious preparations were made for the funeral. All the vehicles in town were hired, all the saloons put in mourning, all the municipal and fire-company flags hung at half-mast, and all the firemen ordered to muster in uniform and bring their machines duly draped in black. Now—let us remark in parenthesis—as all the peoples of the earth had representative adventurers in the Silverland, and as each adventurer had brought the slang of his nation or his locality with him, the combination made the slang of Nevada the richest and the most infinitely varied and copious that had ever existed anywhere in the world, perhaps, except in the mines of California in the "early days." Slang was the language of Nevada. It was hard to preach a sermon without it, and be understood. Such phrases as "You bet!" "Oh, no, I reckon not!" "No Irish need apply," and a hundred others, became so common as to fall from the lips of a speaker unconsciously—and very often when they did not touch the subject under discussion and consequently failed to mean anything.

After Buck Fanshaw's inquest a meeting of the short-haired brotherhood was held, for nothing can be done on the Pacific coast without a public meeting and an expression of sentiment. Regretful resolutions were passed and various committees appointed; among others, a committee of one was deputed to call on the minister, a fragile, gentle, spiritual new fledgling from an Eastern theological seminary, and as yet unacqainted with the ways of the mines. The committeeman, "Scotty" Briggs, made his visit; and in after days it was worth something to hear the minister tell about it. Scotty was a stalwart rough, whose customary suit, when on weighty official business like committee work, was a fire helmet, flaming red flannel shirt, patent leather belt with spanner and revolver attached, coat hung over arm, and pants stuffed into boot tops. He formed something of a contrast to the pale theological student. It is fair to say of Scotty, however, in passing, that he had a warm heart, and a strong love for his friends, and never entered into a quarrel when he could reasonably keep out of it. Indeed it was commonly said that whenever one of Scotty's fights was investigated, it always turned out that it had originally been no affair of his, but that out of native good-heartedness he had dropped in of his own accord to help the man who was getting the worst of it. He and Buck Fanshaw were bosom friends, for years, and had often taken adventurous "pot-luck" together. On one occasion, they had thrown off their coats and taken the weaker side in a fight among strangers, and after gaining a hard-earned victory, turned and found that the men they were helping had deserted early, and not only that, but had stolen their coats and made off with them! But to return to Scotty's visit to the minister. He was on a sorrowful mission, now, and his face was the picture of woe. Being admitted to the presence he sat down before the clergyman, placed his fire-hat on an unfinished manuscript sermon under the minister's nose, took from it a red silk handkerchief, wiped his brow and heaved a sigh of dismal impressiveness, explanatory of his business. He choked, and even shed tears; but with an effort he mastered his voice and said in lugubrious tones:

"Are you the duck that runs the gospel-mill next door?"

"Am I the—pardon me, I believe I do not understand?"

With another sigh and a half-sob, Scotty rejoined:

"Why you see we are in a bit of trouble, and the boys thought maybe you would give us a lift, if we'd tackle you—that is, if I've got the rights of it and you are the head clerk of the doxology-works next door."

"I am the shepherd in charge of the flock whose fold is next door."

"The which?"

"The spiritual adviser of the little company of believers whose sanctuary adjoins these premises."

Scotty scratched his head, reflected a moment, and then said:

"You ruther hold over me, pard. I reckon I can't call that hand. Ante and pass the buck."

"How? I beg pardon. What did I understand you to say?"

"Well, you've ruther got the bulge on me. Or maybe we've both got the bulge, somehow. You don't smoke me and I don't smoke you. You see, one of the boys has passed in his checks and we want to give him a good send-off, and so the thing I'm on now is to roust out somebody to jerk a little chin-music for us and waltz him through handsome."

"My friend, I seem to grow more and more bewildered. Your observations are wholly incomprehensible to me. Cannot you simplify them in some way? At first I thought perhaps I understood you, but I grope now. Would it not expedite matters if you restricted yourself to categorical statements of fact unencumbered with obstructing accumulations of metaphor and allegory?"

Another pause, and more reflection. Then, said Scotty:

"I'll have to pass, I judge."

"How?"

"You've raised me out, pard."

"I still fail to catch your meaning."

"Why, that last lead of yourn is too many for me—that's the idea. I can't neither trump nor follow suit."

The clergyman sank back in his chair perplexed. Scotty leaned his head on his hand and gave himself up to thought. Presently his face came up, sorrowful but confident.

"I've got it now, so's you can savvy," he said. "What we want is a gospel-sharp. See?"

"A what?"

" Gospel-sharp. Parson."

"Oh! Why did you not say so before? I am a clergyman—a parson."

"Now you talk! You see my blind and straddle it like a man. Put it there!"—extending a brawny paw, which closed over the minister's small hand and gave it a shake indicative of fraternal sympathy and fervent gratification.

"Now we're all right, pard. Let's start fresh. Don't

you mind my snuffling a little—becuz we're in a power of trouble. You see, one of the boys has gone up the flume—"

"Gone where?"

"Up the flume—throwed up the sponge, you understand."

"Thrown up the sponge?"

"Yes—kicked the bucket—"

"Ah—has departed to that mysterious country from whose bourne no traveler returns."

"Return! I reckon not. Why pard, he's *dead!*"

"Yes, I understand."

"Oh, you do? Well I thought maybe you might be getting tangled some more. Yes, you see he's dead again—"

"*Again ?* Why, has he ever been dead before?"

"Dead before? No! Do you reckon a man has got as many lives as a cat? But you bet you he's awful dead now, poor old boy, and I wish I'd never seen this day. I don't want no better friend than Buck Fanshaw. I knowed him by the back; and when I know a man and like him, I freeze to him—you hear *me*. Take him all round, pard, there never was a bullier man in the mines. No man ever knowed Buck Fanshaw to go back on a friend. But it's all up, you know, it's all up. It ain't no use. They've scooped him."

"Scooped him?"

"Yes—death has. Well, well, well, we've got to give him up. Yes indeed. It's a kind of a hard world, after all, *ain't* it? But pard, he was a rustler! You ought to seen him get started once. He was a bully boy with a glass eye! Just spit in his face and give him room according to his strength, and it was just beautiful to see him peel and go in. He was the worst son of a thief that ever drawed breath. Pard, he was *on* it! He was on it bigger than an Injun!"

"On it? On what?"

"On the shoot. On the shoulder. On the fight, you understand. *He* didn't give a continental for *any*body. *Beg* your pardon, friend, for coming so near saying a cuss-word—but you see I'm on an awful strain, in this palaver, on account of having to cramp down and draw everything so mild. But we've got to give him up. There ain't any getting around that, I don't reckon. Now if we can get you to help plant him—"

"Preach the funeral discourse? Assist at the obsequies?"

"Obs'quies is good. Yes. That's it—that's our little game. We are going to get the thing up regardless, you know. He was always nifty himself, and so you bet you his funeral ain't going to be no slouch—solid silver door-plate on his coffin, six plumes on the hearse, and a nigger on the box in a biled shirt and a plug hat—how's that for high? And we'll take care of *you*, pard. We'll fix you all right. There'll be a kerridge for you; and whatever you want, you just 'scape out and we'll 'tend to it. We've got a shebang fixed up for you to stand behind, in No. 1's house, and don't you be afraid. Just go in and toot your horn, if you don't sell a clam. Put Buck through as bully as you can, pard, for anybody that knowed him will tell you that he was one of the whitest men that was ever in the mines. You can't draw it too strong. He never could stand it to see things going wrong. He's done more to make this town quiet and peaceable than any man in it. I've seen him lick four

Greasers in eleven minutes, myself. If a thing wanted regulating, *he* warn't a man to go browsing around after somebody to do it, but he would prance in and regulate it himself. He warn't a Catholic. Scasely. He was down on 'em. His word was, 'No Irish need apply!' But it didn't make no difference about that when it came down to what a man's rights was—and so, when some roughs jumped the Catholic bone-yard and started in to stake out town-lots in it he *went* for 'em! And he *cleaned* 'em, too! I was there, pard, and I seen it myself."

"That was very well indeed—at least the impulse was—whether the act was strictly defensible or not. Had deceased any religious convictions? That is to say, did he feel a dependence upon, or acknowledge allegiance to a higher power?"

More reflection.

"I reckon you've stumped me again, pard. Could you say it over once more, and say it slow?"

"Well, to simplify it somewhat, was he, or rather had he ever been connected with any organization sequestered from secular concerns and devoted to self-sacrifice in the interests of morality?"

"All down but nine—set 'em up on the other alley, pard."

"What did I understand you to say?"

"Why, you're most too many for me, you know. When you get in with your left I hunt grass every time. Every time you draw, you fill; but I don't seem to have any luck. Let's have a new deal."

"How? Begin again?"

"That's it."

"Very well. Was he a good man, and—"

"There—I see that; don't put up another chip till I look at my hand. A good man, says you? Pard, it ain't no name for it. He was the best man that ever—pard, you would have doted on that man. He could lam any galoot of his inches in America. It was him that put down the riot last election before it got a start; and everybody said he was the only man that could have done it. He waltzed in with a spanner in one hand and a trumpet in the other, and sent fourteen men home on a shutter in less than three minutes. He had that riot all broke up and prevented nice before anybody ever got a chance to strike a blow. He was always for peace, and he would *have* peace—he could not stand disturbances. Pard, he was a great loss to this town. It would please the boys if you could chip in something like that and do him justice. Here once when the Micks got to throwing stones through the Methodis' Sunday school windows, Buck Fanshaw, all of his own notion, shut up his saloon and took a couple of six-shooters and mounted guard over the Sunday school. Says he, 'No Irish need apply!' And they didn't. He was the bulliest man in the mountains, pard! He could run faster, jump higher, hit harder, and hold more tangle-foot whisky without spilling it than any man in seventeen counties. Put that in, pard—it'll please the boys more than anything you could say. And you can say, pard, that he never shook his mother."

"Never shook his mother?"

"That's it—any of the boys will tell you so."

"Well, but why *should* he shake her?"

"That's what *I* say—but some people does."

"Not people of any repute?"

"Well, some that averages pretty so-so."

"In my opinion the man that would offer personal violence to his own mother, ought to—"

"Cheese it, pard; you've banked your ball clean outside the string. What I was a drivin' at, was, that he never *throwed off* on his mother—don't you see? No indeedy. He give her a house to live in, and town lots, and plenty of money; and he looked after her and took care of her all the time; and when she was down with the small-pox I'm d—d if he didn't set up nights and nuss her himself! *Beg* your pardon for saying it, but it hopped out too quick for yours truly. You've treated me like a gentleman, pard, and I ain't the man to hurt your feelings intentional. I think you're white. I think you're a square man, pard. I like you, and I'll lick any man that don't. I'll lick him till he can't tell himself from a last year's corpse! Put it *there!*" [Another fraternal hand-shake—and exit.]

The obsequies were all that "the boys" could desire. Such a marvel of funeral pomp had never been seen in Virginia. The plumed hearse, the dirge-breathing brass brands, the closed marts of business, the flags drooping at half mast, the long, plodding procession of uniformed secret societies, military battalions and fire companies, draped engines, carriages of officials, and citizens in vehicles and on foot, attracted multitudes of spectators to the sidewalks, roofs, and windows, and for years afterward, the degree of grandeur attained by any civic display in Virginia was determined by comparison with Buck Fanshaw's funeral.

Scotty Briggs, as a pall-hearer and a mourner, occupied a prominent place at the funeral, and when the sermon was finished and the last sentence of the prayer for the dead man's soul ascended, he responded, in a low voice, but with feeling:

"AMEN. No Irish need apply."

As the hulk of the response was without apparent relevancy, it was probably nothing more than a humble tribute to the memory of the friend that was gone; for, as Scotty had once said, it was " his word."

Scotty Briggs, in after days, achieved the distinction of becoming the only convert to religion that was ever gathered from the Virginia roughs; and it transpired that the man who had it in him to espouse the quarrel of the weak out of inborn nobility of spirit was no mean timber whereof to construct a Christian. The making him one did not warp his generosity or diminish his courage; on the contrary it gave intelligent direction to the one and a broader field to the other. If his Sunday-school class progressed faster than the other classes, was it matter for wonder? I think not. He talked to his pioneer small-fry in a language they understood! It was my large privilege, a month before he died, to hear him tell the beautiful story of Joseph and his brethren to his class "without looking at the book." I leave it to the reader to fancy what it was like, as it fell, riddled with slang, from the lips of that grave, earnest teacher, and was listened to by his little learners with a consuming interest that showed that they were as unconscious as he was that any violence was being done to the sacred proprieties!

from *Roughing It*, 1872

The Great Land-slide Case

THE mountains are very high and steep about Carson, Eagle and Washoe Valleys—very high and very steep, and so when the snow gets to melting off fast in the Spring and the warm surface-earth begins to moisten and soften, the disastrous land-slides commence. The reader cannot know what a land-slide is, unless he has lived in that country and seen the whole side of a mountain taken off some fine morning and deposited down in the valley, leaving a vast, treeless, unsightly scar upon the mountain's front to keep the circumstance fresh in his memory all the years that he may go on living within seventy miles of that place.

General Buncombe was shipped out to Nevada in the invoice of Territorial officers, to be United States Attorney. He considered himself a lawyer of parts, and he very much wanted an opportunity to manifest it—partly for the pure gratification of it and partly because his salary was Territorially meagre (which is a strong expression). Now the older citizens of a new territory look down upon the rest of the world with a calm, benevolent compassion, as long as it keeps out of the way—when it gets in the way they snub it. Sometimes this latter takes the shape of a practical joke.

One morning Dick Hyde rode furiously up to

General Buncombe's door in Carson city and rushed into his presence without stopping to tie his horse. He seemed much excited. He told the General that he wanted him to conduct a suit for him and would pay him five hundred dollars if he achieved a victory. And then, with violent gestures and a world of profanity, he poured out his griefs. He said it was pretty well known that for some years he had been farming (or ranching as the more customary term is) in Washoe District, and making a successful thing of it, and furthermore it was known that his ranch was situated just in the edge of the valley, and that Tom Morgan owned a ranch immediately above it on the mountain side. And now time trouble was, that one of those hated and dreaded land-slides had come and slid Morgan's ranch, fences, cabins, cattle, barns and everything down on top of *his* ranch and exactly covered up every single vestige of his property, to a depth of about thirty-eight feet. Morgan was in possession and refused to vacate the premises—said he was occupying his own cabin and not interfering with anybody else's—and said the cabin was standing on the same dirt and same ranch it had always stood on, and he would like to see anybody make him vacate.

"And when I reminded him," said Hyde, weeping, "that it was on top of my ranch and that he was trespassing, he had the infernal meanness to ask me why didn't I *stay* on my ranch and hold possession when I see him a-coming! Why didn't I *stay* on it, the blathering lunatic—by George, when I heard that racket and looked up that hill it was just like the whole world was a-ripping and a-tearing down that mountain side—splinters, and cord-wood, thunder and lightning, hail and snow, odds and ends of hay stacks, and awful clouds of dust!—trees going end over end in the air, rocks as big as a house jumping 'bout a thousand feet high and busting into ten million pieces, cattle turned inside out and a-coming head on with their tails hanging out between their teeth!—and in the midst of all that wrack and destruction sot that cussed Morgan on his gate-post, a-wondering why I didn't *stay and hold possession!* Laws bless me, I just took one glimpse, General, and lit out'n the county in three jumps exactly.

"But what grinds me is that that Morgan hangs on there and won't move off'n that ranch—says it's his'n and he's going to keep it—likes it better'n he did when it was higher up the hill. Mad! Well, I've been so mad for two days I couldn't find my way to town—been wandering around in the brush in a starving condition—got anything here to drink, General? But I'm here *now*, and I'm a-going to law. You hear *me!*"

Never in all the world, perhaps, were a man's feelings so outraged as were the General's. He said he had never heard of such high-handed conduct in all his life as this Morgan's. And he said there was no use in going to law—Morgan had no shadow of right to remain where he was—nobody in the wide world would uphold him in it, and no lawyer would take his case and no judge listen to it. Hyde said that right there was where he was mistaken—everybody in town sustained Morgan; Hal Brayton, a very smart lawyer, had taken his case; the courts being in vacation, it was to be tried before a referee, and ex-Governor Roop had already been appointed to that office and would open his court in a large public hall near the hotel at two that afternoon.

The General was amazed. He said he had suspected before that the people of that Territory were fools, and now he knew it. But he said rest easy, rest easy and collect the witnesses, for the victory was just as certain as if the conflict were already over. Hyde wiped away his tears and left.

At two in the afternoon referee Roop's Court opened, and Roop appeared throned among his sheriffs, the witnesses, and spectators, and wearing upon his face a solemnity so awe-inspiring that some of his fellow-conspirators had misgivings that maybe he had not comprehended, after all, that this was merely a joke. An unearthly stillness prevailed, for at the slightest noise the judge uttered sternly the command:

"Order in the Court!"

And the sheriffs promptly echoed it. Presently the General elbowed his way through the crowd of spectators, with his arms full of law-books, and on his ears fell an order from the judge which was the first respectful recognition of his high official dignity that had ever saluted them, and it trickled pleasantly through his whole system:

"Way for the United States Attorney!"

The witnesses were called—legislators, high government officers, ranchmen, miners, Indians, Chinamen, negroes. Three fourths of them were called by the defendant Morgan, but no matter, their testimony invariably went in favor of the plaintiff Hyde. Each new witness only added new testimony to the absurdity of a man's claiming to own another man's property because his farm had slid down on top of it. Then the Morgan lawyers made their speeches, and seemed to make singularly weak ones—they did really nothing to help the Morgan cause. And now the General, with exultation in his face, got up and made an impassioned effort; he pounded the table, he banged the law-books, he shouted, and roared, and howled, he quoted from everything and everybody, poetry, sarcasm, statistics, history, pathos, bathos, blasphemy, and wound up with a grand war-whoop for free speech, freedom of the press, free schools, the Glorious Bird of America and the principles of eternal justice! [Applause.]

When the General sat down, he did it with the conviction that if there was anything in good strong testimony, a great speech and believing and admiring countenances all around, Mr. Morgan's case was killed. Ex-Governor Roop leant his head upon his hand for some minutes, thinking, and the still audience waited for his decision. Then he got up and stood erect, with bended head, and thought again. Then he walked the floor with long, deliberate strides, his chin in his hand, and still the audience waited. At last he returned to his throne, seated himself, and began, impressively:

"Gentlemen, I feel the great responsibility that rests upon me this day. This is no ordinary case. On the contrary it is plain that it is the most solemn and awful that ever man was called upon to decide. Gentlemen, I have listened attentively to the evidence, and have perceived that the weight of it, the overwhelming weight of it, is in favor of the plaintiff Hyde. I have listened also to the remarks of counsel, with high interest—and especially will I commend the masterly and irrefutable logic of the distinguished gentleman who represents the plaintiff. But gentlemen, let us beware how we allow mere human testimony, human ingenuity in argument and human ideas of equity, to influence us at a moment so solemn as this. Gentlemen, it ill becomes us, worms as we are, to meddle with the decrees of Heaven. It is plain to me that Heaven, in its inscrutable wisdom, has seen fit to move this defendant's ranch for a purpose. We are but creatures, and we must submit. If Heaven has chosen to favor the defendant Morgan in this marked and wonderful manner; and if Heaven, dissatisfied with the position of the Morgan ranch upon the mountain side, has chosen to remove it to a position more eligible and more advantageous for its owner, it ill becomes us, insects as we are, to question the legality of the act or inquire into the reasons that prompted it. No—Heaven created the ranches and it is Heaven's prerogative to rearrange them, to experiment with them, to shift them around at its pleasure. It is for us to submit, without repining. I warn you that this thing which has happened is a thing with which the sacrilegious hands and brains and tongues of men must not meddle. Gentlemen, it is the verdict of this court that the plaintiff, Richard Hyde, has been deprived of his ranch by the visitation of God! And from this decision there is no appeal."

Buncombe seized his cargo of law-books and plunged out of the court-room frantic with indignation. He pronounced Roop to be a miraculous fool, an inspired idiot. In all good faith he returned at night and remonstrated with Roop upon his extravagant decision, and implored him to walk the floor and think for half an hour, and see if he could not figure out some sort of modification of the verdict. Roop yielded at last and got up to walk. He walked two hours and a half, and at last his face lit up happily and he told Buncombe it had occurred to him that the ranch underneath the new Morgan ranch still belonged to Hyde, that his title to the ground was just as good as it had ever been, and therefore he was of opinion that Hyde had a right to dig it out from under there and—

The General never waited to hear the end of it. He was always an impatient and irascible man, that way. At the end of two months the fact that he had been played upon with a joke had managed to bore itself, like another Hoosac Tunnel, through the solid adamant of his understanding.

from *Roughing It*, 1872

His Grandfather's Old Ram

EVERY now and then, in these days, the boys used to tell me I ought to get one Jim Blaine to tell me the stirring story of his grandfather's old ram—but they always added that I must not mention the matter unless Jim was drunk at the time—just comfortably and sociably drunk. They kept this up until my curiosity was on the rack to hear the story. I got to haunting Blaine; but it was of no use, the boys always found fault with his condition; he was often moderately but never satis-factorily drunk. I never watched a man's condition with such absorbing interest, such anxious solicitude; I never so pined to see a man uncompromisingly drunk before. At last, one evening I hurried to his cabin, for I learned that this time his situation was such that even the most fastidious could find no fault with it—he was tranquilly, serenely, symmetrically drunk—not a hiccup to mar his voice, not a cloud upon his brain thick enough to obscure his memory. As I entered, he was sitting upon an empty powder-keg, with a clay pipe in one hand and the other raised to command silence. His face was round, red, and very serious; his throat was bare and his hair tumbled; in general appearance and costume he was a stalwart miner of the period. On the pine table stood a candle, and its dim light revealed "the boys" sitting here and there on bunks, candle-boxes, powder-kegs, etc. They said:

"Sh—! Don't speak—he's going to commence."

THE STORY OF THE OLD RAM.

I found a seat at once, and Blaine said:

"I don't reckon them times will ever come again. There never was a more bullier old ram than what he was. Grandfather fetched him from Illinois—got him of a man by the name of Yates—Bill Yates—maybe you might have heard of him; his father was a deacon—Baptist—and he was a rustler, too; a man had to get up ruther early to get the start of old Thankful Yates; it was him that put the Greens up to jining teams with my grandfather when he moved west. Seth Green was prob'ly the pick of the flock he married a Wilkerson—Sarah Wilkerson—good cretur, she was—one of the likeliest heifers that was ever raised in old Stoddard, everybody said that knowed her. She could heft a bar'l of flour as easy as I can flirt a flapjack. And spin? Don't mention it! Independent? Humph! When Sile Hawkins come a browsing around her, she let him know that for all his tin he couldn't trot in harness alongside of *her*. You see, Sile Hawkins was—no, it warn't Sile Hawkins, after all—it was a galoot by the name of Filkins—I disremember his first name; but he *was* a stump—come into pra'r meeting drunk, one night, hooraying for Nixon, becuz he thought it was a primary; and old deacon Ferguson up and scooted him through the window and he lit on old Miss Jefferson's head, poor old filly. She was a good soul—had a glass eye and used to lend it to old Miss Wagner, that hadn't any, to receive company in; it warn't big enough, and when Miss Wagner warn't noticing, it would get twisted around in the socket, and look up, maybe, or out to one side, and every which way, while t'other one was looking as straight ahead as a spy-glass. Grown people didn't mind it, but it most always made the children cry, it was so sort of scary. She tried packing it in raw cotton, but it wouldn't work, somehow—the cotton would get loose and stick out and look so kind of awful that the children couldn't stand it no way. She was always dropping it out, and turning up her old dead-light on the company empty, and making them oncomfortable, becuz *she* never could tell when it hopped out, being blind on that side, you see. So somebody would have to hunch her and say, "Your game eye has fetched loose, Miss Wagner dear"—and then all of them would have to sit and wait till she jammed it in again—wrong side before, as a general thing, and green as a bird's egg, being a bashful cretur and easy sot back before company. But being wrong side before warn't much difference, anyway, becuz her own eye was sky-blue and the glass one was yaller on the front side, so whichever way she turned it it didn't match nohow. Old Miss Wagner was considerable on the borrow, she was. When she had a quilting, or Dorcas S'iety at her house she gen'ally borrowed Miss Higgins's wooden leg to stump around on; it was considerable shorter than her other pin, but much *she* minded that. She said she couldn't abide crutches when she had company, becuz they were so slow; said when she had company and things had to be done, she wanted to get up and hump herself. She was as bald as a jug, and so she used to borrow Miss Jacops's wig—Miss Jacops was the coffin-peddler's wife—a ratty old buzzard, he was, that used to go roosting around where people was sick, waiting for 'em; and there that old rip would sit all day, in the shade, on a coffin that he judged would fit the can'idate; and if it was a slow customer and kind of uncertain, he'd fetch his rations and a blanket along and sleep in the coffin nights. He was anchored out that way, in frosty weather, for about three weeks, once, before old Robbins's place, waiting for him; and after that, for as much as two years, Jacops was not on speaking terms with the old man, on account of his disapp'inting him. He got one of his feet froze, and lost money, too, becuz old Robbins took a favorable turn and got well. The next time Robbins got sick, Jacops tried to make up with him, and varnished up the same old coffin and fetched it along; but old Robbins was too many for him; he had him in, and 'peared to be powerful weak; he bought the coffin for ten dollars and Jacops was to pay it back and twenty-five more besides if Robbins didn't like the coffin after he'd tried it. And then Robbins died, and at the funeral he bursted off the lid and riz up in his shroud and told the parson to let up on the performances, becuz he could *not* stand such a coffin as that. You see he had been in a trance once before, when he was young, and he took the chances on another, cal'lating that if he made the trip it was money in his pocket, and if he missed fire he couldn't lose a cent. And by George he sued Jacops for the rhino and got jedgment; and he set up the coffin in his back parlor and said he 'lowed to take his time, now. It was always an aggravation to Jacops, the way that miserable old thing acted. He moved back to Indiany pretty soon—went to

Wellsville—Wellsville was the place the Hogadorns was from. Mighty fine family. Old Maryland stock. Old Squire Hogadorn could carry around more mixed licker, and cuss better than most any man I ever see. His second wife was the widder Billings—she that was Becky Martin; her dam was deacon Dunlap's first wife. Her oldest child, Maria, married a missionary and died in grace—et up by the savages. They et *him*, too, poor feller—biled him. It warn't the custom, so they say, but they explained to friends of his'n that went down there to bring away his things, that they'd tried missionaries every other way and never could get any good out of 'em—and so it annoyed all his relations to find out that that man's life was fooled away just out of a dern'd experiment, so to speak. But mind you, there ain't anything ever reely lost; everything that people can't understand and don't see the reason of does good if you only hold on and give it a fair shake; Prov'dence don't fire no blank ca'tridges, boys. That there missionary's substance, unbeknowns to himself, actu'ly converted every last one of them heathens that took a chance at the barbacue. Nothing ever fetched them but that. Don't tell *me* it was an accident that he was biled. There ain't no such a thing as an accident. When my Uncle Lem was leaning up agin a scaffolding once, sick, or drunk, or suthin, an Irishman with a hod full of bricks fell on him out of the third story and broke the old man's back in two places. People said it was an accident. Much accident there was about that. He didn't know what he was there for, but he was there for a good object. If he hadn't been there the Irishman would have been killed. Nobody can ever make me believe anything different from that. Uncle Lem's dog was there. Why didn't the Irishman fall on the dog? Becuz the dog would a seen him a coming and stood from under. That's the reason the dog warn't appinted. A dog can't be depended on to carry out a special providence. Mark my words it was a put-up thing. Accidents don't happen, boys. Uncle Lem's dog—I wish you could a seen that dog. He was a reglar shepherd—or ruther he was part bull and part shepherd—splendid animal; belonged to parson Hagar before Uncle Lem got him. Parson Hagar belonged to the Western Reserve Hagars; prime family; his mother was a Watson; one of his sisters married a Wheeler; they settled in Morgan county, and he got nipped by the machinery in a carpet factory and went through in less than a quarter of a minute; his widder bought the piece of carpet that had his remains wove in, and people come a hundred mile to 'tend the funeral. There was fourteen yards in the piece. She wouldn't let them roll him up, but planted him just so—full length. The church was middling small where they preached the funeral, and they had to let one end of the coffin stick out of the window. They didn't bury him—they planted one end, and let him stand up, same as a monument. And they nailed a sign on it and put—put on—put on it—sacred to—the m-e-m-o-r-y—of fourteen y-a-r-d-s—of three-ply—car - - -pet—containing all that was—m-o-r-t-a-l—of—of—W-i-l-l-i-a-m—W-h-e—"

Jim Blaine had been growing gradually drowsy and drowsier—his head nodded, once, twice, three times—dropped peacefully upon his breast, and he fell tranquilly asleep. The tears were running down the boys' cheeks—they were suffocating with suppressed laughter—and had been from the start, though I had never noticed it. I perceived that I was "sold." I learned then that Jim Blaine's peculiarity was that whenever he reached a certain stage of intoxication, no human power could keep him from setting out, with impressive unction, to tell about a wonderful adventure which he had once had with his grandfather's old ram—and the mention of the ram in the first sentence was as far as any man had ever heard him get, concerning it. He always maundered off, interminably, from one thing to another, till his whisky got the best of him and he fell asleep. What the thing was that happened to him and his grandfather's old ram is a dark mystery to this day, for nobody has ever yet found out.

from *Roughing It*, 1872

Experience of the McWilliamses with Membranous Croup

[*As related to the author of this book by Mr. McWilliams, a pleasant New York gentleman whom the said author met by chance on a journey.*]

WELL, to go back to where I was before I digressed to explain to you how that frightful and incurable disease, membranous croup, was ravaging the town and driving all mothers mad with terror, I called Mrs. McWilliams's attention to little Penelope and said:

"Darling, I wouldn't let that child be chewing that pine stick if I were you."

"Precious, where is the harm in it?" said she, but at the same time preparing to take away the stick—for women cannot receive even the most palpably judicious suggestion without arguing it; that is, married women.

I replied:

"Love, it is notorious that pine is the least nutritious wood that a child can eat."

My wife's hand paused, in the act of taking the stick, and returned itself to her lap. She bridled perceptibly, and said:

"Hubby, you know better than that. You know you do. Doctors *all* say that the turpentine in pine wood is good for weak back and the kidneys."

"Ah—I was under a misapprehension. I did not know that the child's kidneys and spine were affected, and that the family physician had recommended—"

"Who said the child's spine and kidneys were affected?"

"My love, you intimated it."

"The idea! I never intimated anything of the kind."

"Why my dear, it hasn't been two minutes since you said—"

"Bother what I said! I don't care what I did say. There isn't any harm in the child's chewing a bit of pine stick if she wants to, and you know it perfectly well. And she *shall* chew it, too. So there, now!"

"Say no more, my dear. I now see the force of your reasoning, and I will go and order two or three cords of the best pine wood to-day. No child of mine shall want while I—"

"O *please* go along to your office and let me have some peace. A body can never make the simplest remark but you must take it up and go to arguing and arguing and arguing till you don't know what you are talking about, and you *never* do."

"Very well, it shall be as you say. But there is a want of logic in your last remark which—"

However, she was gone with a flourish before I could finish, and had taken the child with her. That night at dinner she confronted me with a face as white as a sheet:

"O, Mortimer, there's another! Little Georgie Gordon is taken."

"Membranous croup?"

"Membranous croup."

"Is there any hope for him?"

"None in the wide world. O, what is to become of us!"

By and by a nurse brought in our Penelope to say good-night and offer the customary prayer at the mother's knee. In the midst of "Now I lay me down to sleep," she gave a slight cough! My wife fell back like one stricken with death. But the next moment she was up and brimming with the activities which terror inspires.

She commanded that the child's crib be removed from the nursery to our bed-room; and she went along to see the order executed. She took me with her, of course. We got matters arranged with speed. A cot bed was put up in my wife's dressing room for the nurse. But now Mrs. McWilliams said we were too far away from the other baby, and what if *he* were to have the symptoms in the night—and she blanched again, poor thing.

We then restored the crib and the nurse to the nursery and put up a bed for ourselves in a room adjoining.

Presently, however, Mrs. McWilliams said suppose the baby should catch it from Penelope? This thought struck a new panic to her heart, and the tribe of us could not get the crib out of the nursery again fast enough to satisfy my wife, though she assisted in her own person and well nigh pulled the crib to pieces in her frantic hurry.

We moved down stairs; but there was no place there to stow the nurse, and Mrs. McWilliams said the nurse's experience would be an inestimable help. So we returned, bag and baggage, to our own bed-room once more, and felt a great gladness, like storm-buffeted birds that have found their nest again.

Mrs. McWilliams sped to the nursery to see how things were going on there. She was back in a moment with a new dread. She said:

"What *can* make Baby sleep so?"

I said:

"Why, my darling, Baby *always* sleeps like a graven image."

"I know. I know; but there's something peculiar about his sleep, now. He seems to—to—he seems to breathe so *regularly*. O, this is dreadful."

"But my dear he always breathes regularly."

"Oh, I know it, but there's something frightful about it now. His nurse is too young and inexperienced. Maria shall stay there with her, and be on hand if anything happens."

"That is a good idea, but who will help *you?*"

"You can help me all I want. I wouldn't allow anybody to do anything but myself, any how, at such a time as this."

I said I would feel mean to lie abed and sleep, and leave her to watch and toil over our little patient all the weary night.—But she reconciled me to it. So old Maria departed and took up her ancient quarters in the nursery.

Penelope coughed twice in her sleep.

"Oh, why *don't* that doctor come! Mortimer, this room is too warm. This room is certainly too warm. Turn off the register—quick!"

I shut it off, glancing at the thermometer at the same time, and wondering to myself if 70 *was* too warm for a sick child.

The coachman arrived from down town, now, with the news that our physician was ill and confined to his bed.—Mrs. McWilliams turned a dead eye upon me, and said in a dead voice:

"There is a Providence in it. It is foreordained. He never was sick before.—Never. We have not been living as we ought to live, Mortimer. Time and time again I have told you so. Now you see the result. Our child will never get well. Be thankful if you can forgive yourself; I never can forgive *myself*."

I said, without intent to hurt, but with heedless choice of words, that I could not see that we had been living such an abandoned life.

"*Mortimer!* Do you want to bring the judgment upon Baby, too!"

Then she began to cry, but suddenly exclaimed:

"The doctor must have sent medicines!"

I said:

"Certainly. They are here. I was only waiting for you to give me a chance."

"Well do give them to me! Don't you know that every moment is precious now? But what was the use in sending medicines, when he *knows* that the disease is incurable?"

I said that while there was life there was hope.

"Hope! Mortimer, you know no more what you are talking about than the child unborn. If you would—. As I live, the directions say give one teaspoonful once an hour! Once an hour!—as if we had a whole year before us to save the child in! Mortimer, please hurry. Give the poor perishing thing a table-spoonful, and *try* to be quick!"

"Why, my dear, a table-spoonful might—"

"*Don't* drive me frantic!...There, there, there, my precious, my own; it's nasty bitter stuff, but it's good for Nelly—good for Mother's precious darling; and it will make her well. There, there, there, put the little head on Mamma's breast and go to sleep, and pretty soon—Oh, I know she can't live till morning! Mortimer, a table-spoonful every half hour will—. Oh, the child needs belladonna too; I know she does—and aconite. Get them, Mortimer. Now do let me have my way. You know nothing about these things."

We now went to bed, placing the crib close to my wife's pillow. All this turmoil had worn upon me, and within two minutes I was something more than half asleep. Mrs. McWilliams roused me:

"Darling, is that register turned on?"

"No."

" I thought as much. Please turn it on at once. This room is cold."

I turned it on, and presently fell asleep again. I was aroused once more:

"Dearie, would you mind moving the crib to your side of the bed? It is nearer the register."

I moved it, but had a collision with the rug and woke up the child. I dozed off once more, while my wife quieted the sufferer. But in a little while these words came murmuring remotely through the fog of my drowsiness:

"Mortimer, if we only had some goose-grease—will you ring?"

I climbed dreamily out, and stepped on a cat, which responded with a protest and would have got a convincing kick for it if a chair had not got it instead.

"Now, Mortimer, why do you want to turn up the gas and wake up the child again?"

"Because I want to see how much I am hurt, Caroline."

"Well look at the chair, too—I have no doubt it is ruined. Poor cat, suppose you had—"

"Now I am not going to suppose anything about the cat. It never would have occurred if Maria had been allowed to remain here and attend to these duties, which are in her line and are not in mine."

"Now Mortimer, I should think you would be ashamed to make a remark like that. It is a pity if you cannot do the few little things I ask of you at such an awful time as this when our child—"

"There, there, I will do anything you want. But I can't raise anybody with this bell. They're all gone to bed. Where is the goose-grease?"

"On the mantel piece in the nursery. If you'll step there and speak to Maria—"

I fetched the goose-grease and went to sleep again: Once more I was called:

"Mortimer, I so hate to disturb you, but the room is still too cold for me to try to apply this stuff. Would you mind lighting the fire? It is all ready to touch a match to."

I dragged myself out and lit the fire, and then sat down disconsolate.

"Mortimer, don't sit there and catch your death of cold. Come to bed."

"As I was stepping in, she said:

"But wait a moment. Please give the child some more of the medicine."

Which I did. It was a medicine which made a child more or less lively; so my wife made use of its waking interval to strip it and grease it all over with the goose-oil. I was soon asleep once more, but once more I had to get up.

"Mortimer, I feel a draft. I feel it distinctly. There is nothing so bad for this disease as a draft. Please move the crib in front of the fire."

I did it; and collided with the rug again, which I threw in the fire. Mrs. McWilliams sprang out of bed and rescued it and we had some words. I had another trifling interval of sleep, and then got up, by request, and constructed a flax-seed poultice. This was placed upon the child's breast and left there to do its healing work.

A wood fire is not a permanent thing. I got up every twenty minutes and renewed ours, and this gave Mrs. McWilliams the opportunity to shorten the times of giving the medicines by ten minutes, which was a great satisfaction to her. Now and then, between times, I reorganized the flax-seed poultices, and applied sinapisms and other sorts of blisters where unoccupied places could be found upon the child. Well, toward morning the wood gave out and my wife wanted me to go down cellar and get some more. I said:

"My dear, it is a laborious job, and the child must be nearly warm enough, with her extra clothing. Now mightn't we put on another layer of poultices and—"

I did not finish, because I was interrupted. I lugged wood up from below for some little time, and then turned in and fell to snoring as only a man can whose strength is all gone and whose soul is worn out. Just at broad daylight I felt a grip on my shoulder that brought me to my senses suddenly.—My wife was glaring down upon me and gasping. As soon as she could command her tongue she said:

"It is all over! All over! The child's perspiring! What *shall* we do?"

"Mercy, how you terrify me! *I* don't know what we

ought to do. Maybe if we scraped her and put her in the draft again—"

"O, idiot ! There is not a moment to lose! Go for the doctor. Go yourself. Tell him he *must* come, dead or alive."

I dragged that poor sick man from his bed and brought him. He looked at the child and said she was not dying. This was joy unspeakable to me, but it made my wife as mad as if he had offered her a personal affront. Then he said the child's cough was only caused by some trifling irritation or other in the throat. At this I thought my wife had a mind to show him the door.— Now the doctor said he would make the child cough harder and dislodge the trouble. So he gave her something that sent her into a spasm of coughing, and presently up came a little wood splinter or so."

"This child has no membranous croup," said he. "She has been chewing a bit of pine shingle or something of the kind, and got some little slivers in her throat. They won't do her any hurt."

"No," said I, "I can well believe that. Indeed the turpentine that is in them is very good for certain sorts of diseases that are peculiar to children. My wife will tell you so."

But she did not. She turned away in disdain and left the room; and since that time there is one episode in our life which we never refer to. Hence the tide of our days flows by in deep and untroubled serenity.

[Very few married men have such an experience as McWilliams's, and so the author of this book thought that maybe the novelty of it would give it a passing interest to the reader.]

1875

Mrs. McWilliams and the Lightning

WELL, sir—continued Mr. McWilliams, for this was not the beginning of his talk—the fear of lightning is one of the most distressing infirmities a human being can be afflicted with. It is mostly confined to women; but now and then you find it in a little dog, and sometimes in a man. It is a particularly distressing infirmity, for the reason that it takes the sand out of a person to an extent which no other fear can, and it can't be *reasoned* with, and neither can it be shamed out of a person. A woman who could face the devil himself—or a mouse—loses her grip and goes all to pieces in front of a flash of lightning. Her fright is something pitiful to see.

Well, as I was telling you, I woke up, with that smothered and unlocatable cry of "Mortimer! Mortimer!" wailing in my ears; and as soon as I could scrape my faculties together I reached over in the dark and then said:

"Evangeline, is that you calling? What is the matter? Where are you?"

"Shut up in the boot-closet. You ought to be ashamed to lie there and sleep so, and such an awful storm going on."

"Why, how *can* one be ashamed when he is asleep? It is unreasonable; a man *can't* be ashamed when he is asleep,

Evangeline."

"You never try, Mortimer—you know very well you never try."

I caught the sound of muffled sobs.

That sound smote dead the sharp speech that was on my lips, and I changed it to—

"I'm sorry, dear—I'm truly sorry. I never meant to act so. Come back and—"

"MORTIMER!"

"Heavens! what is the matter, my love?"

"Do you mean to say you are in that bed yet?"

"Why, of course."

"Come out of it instantly. I should think you would take some *little* care of your life, for *my* sake and the children's, if you will not for your own."

"But, my love—"

"Don't talk to me, Mortimer. You *know* there is no place so dangerous as a bed in such a thunder-storm as this—all the books say that; yet there you would lie, and deliberately throw away your life—for goodness knows what, unless for the sake of arguing, and arguing, and—"

"But, confound it, Evangeline, I'm *not* in the bed *now*. I'm—"

[Sentence interrupted by a sudden glare of lightning, followed by a terrified little scream from Mrs. McWilliams and a tremendous blast of thunder.]

"There! You see the result. Oh, Mortimer, how *can* you be so profligate as to swear at such a time as this?"

"I *didn't* swear. And that *wasn't* a result of it, anyway. It would have come, just the same, if I hadn't said a word; and you know very well, Evangeline—at least, you ought to know—that when the atmosphere is charged with electricity—"

"Oh, yes; now argue it, and argue it, and argue it!—I don't see how you can act so, when you *know* there is not a lightning-rod on the place, and your poor wife and children are absolutely at the mercy of Providence. What *are* you doing?—lighting a match at such a time as this! Are you stark mad?"

"Hang it, woman, where's the harm? The place is as dark as the inside of an infidel, and—"

"Put it out! Put it out instantly! Are you determined to sacrifice us all? you *know* there is nothing attracts lightning like a light. [*Fzt!—crash! boom—boloom-boom-boom!*] Oh just hear it! Now you see what you've done!"

"No, I *don't* see what I've done. A match may attract lightning, for all I know, but it don't *cause* lightning—I'll go odds on that. And it didn't attract it worth a cent this time; for if that shot was leveled at my match, it was blessed poor marksmanship—about an average of none out of a possible million, I should say. Why, at Dollymount such marksmanship as that—"

"For shame, Mortimer! Here we are standing right in the very presence of death, and yet in so solemn a moment you are capable of using such language as that. If you have no desire to—Mortimer!"

"Well?"

"Did you say your prayers to-night?"

"I—I—meant to, but I got to trying to cipher out how much twelve times thirteen is, and—"

[*Fzt!—boom-berroom-boom! bumble-umble bang-*SMASH!]

"Oh, we are lost, beyond all help! How *could* you

neglect such a thing at such a time as this?"

"But it *wasn't* 'such a time as this.' There wasn't a cloud in the sky. How could *I* know there was going to be all this rumpus and pow-wow about a little slip like that? And I don't think it's just fair for you to make so much out of it, anyway, seeing it happens so seldom; I haven't missed before since I brought on that earthquake, four years ago."

"MORTIMER! How you talk! Have you forgotten the yellow-fever?"

"My dear, you are always throwing up the yellow-fever to me, and I think it is perfectly unreasonable. You can't even send a telegraphic message as far as Memphis without relays, so how is a little devotional slip of mine going to carry so far? I'll *stand* the earthquake, because it was in the neighborhood; but I'll be hanged if I'm going to be responsible for every blamed—"

[*Ftz!*—BOOM *beroom*-boom! boom.-BANG!]

"Oh, dear, dear, dear! I *know* it struck something, Mortimer. We never shall see the light of another day; and if it will do you any good to remember, when we are gone, that your dreadful language—*Mortimer!*"

"WELL! What now?"

"Your voice sounds as if—Mortimer, are you actually standing in front of that open fireplace?"

"That is the very crime I am committing."

"Get away from it this moment! You do seem determined to bring destruction on us all. Don't you *know* that there is no better conductor for lightning than an open chimney? *Now* where have you got to?"

"I'm here by the window."

"Oh, for pity's sake! have you lost your mind? Clear out from there, this moment! The very children in arms know it is fatal to stand near a window in a thunder-storm. Dear, dear, I know I shall never see the light of another day! Mortimer!"

"Yes."

"What is that rustling?"

"It's me."

"What are you doing?"

"Trying to find the upper end of my pantaloons."

"Quick! throw those things away! I do believe you would deliberately put on those clothes at such a time as this; yet you know perfectly well that *all* authorities agree that woolen stuffs attract lightning. Oh, dear, dear, it isn't sufficient that one's life must be in peril from natural causes, but you must do everything you can possibly think of to augment the danger. Oh, *don't* sing! What *can* you be thinking of?"

"Now where's the harm in it?"

"Mortimer, if I have told you once, I have told you a hundred times, that singing causes vibrations in the atmosphere which interrupt the flow of the electric fluid, and—What on *earth* are you opening that door for?"

"Goodness gracious, woman, is there any harm in *that*?"

"*Harm?* There's *death* in it. Anybody that has given this subject any attention knows that to create a draught is to invite the lightning. You haven't half shut it; shut it *tight*—and do hurry, or we are all destroyed. Oh, it is an awful thing to be shut up with a lunatic at such a time as this. Mortimer, what *are* you doing?"

"Nothing. Just turning on the water. This room is

smothering hot and close. I want to bathe my face and hands."

"You have certainly parted with the remnant of your mind! Where lightning strikes any other substance once, it strikes water fifty times. Do turn it off. Oh, dear, I am sure that nothing in this world can save us. It does seem to me that—Mortimer, what was that?"

"It was a da—it was a picture. Knocked it down."

"Then you are close to the wall! I never heard of such imprudence! Don't you *know* that there's no better conductor for lightning than a wall? Come away from there! And you came as near as anything to swearing, too. Oh, how can you be so desperately wicked, and your family in such peril? Mortimer, did you order a feather bed, as I asked you to do?"

"No. Forgot it."

"Forgot it! It may cost you your life. If you had a feather bed now, and could spread it in the middle of the room and lie on it, you would be perfectly safe. Come in here—come quick, before you have a chance to commit any more frantic indiscretions."

I tried, but the little closet would not hold us both with the door shut, unless we could be content to smother. I gasped awhile, then forced my way out. My wife called out:

"Mortimer, something *must* be done for your preservation. Give me that German book that is on the end of the mantelpiece, and a candle; but don't light it; give me a match; I will light it in here. That book has some directions in it."

I got the book—at cost of a vase and some other brittle things; and the madam shut herself up with her candle. I had a moment's peace; then she called out:

"Mortimer, what was that?"

"Nothing but the cat."

"The cat! Oh, destruction! Catch her, and shut her up in the washstand. Do be quick, love; cats are *full* of electricity. I just know my hair will turn white with this night's awful perils."

I heard the muffled sobbings again. But for that, I should not have moved hand or foot in such a wild enterprise in the dark.

However, I went at my task—over chairs, and against all sorts of obstructions, all of them hard ones, too, and most of them with sharp edge—and at last I got kitty cooped up in the commode, at an expense of over four hundred dollars in broken furniture and shins. Then these muffled words came from the closet:

"It says the safest thing is to stand on a chair in the middle of the room, Mortimer; and the legs of the chair must be insulated with non-conductors. That is, you must set the legs of the chair in glass tumblers. [*Fzt!—boom—bang!—smash*!] Oh, hear that! Do hurry, Mortimer, before you are struck."

I managed to find and secure the tumblers. I got the last four—broke all the rest. I insulated the chair legs, and called for further instructions.

"Mortimer, it says, 'Während eines Gewitters entferne man Metalle, wie z. B., Ringe, Uhren, Schlüssel, etc., von sich und halte sich auch nicht an solchen Stellen auf, wo viele Metalle bei einander liegen, oder mit andern Körpern verbunden sind, wie an Herden, Oefen, Elsengittern u. dgl.' What does that mean, Mortimer? Does it mean that you must keep metals *about* you, or keep them *away* from you?"

"Well, I hardly know. It appears to be a little mixed. All German advice is more or less mixed. However, I think that that sentence is mostly in the dative case, with a little genitive and accusative sifted in, here and there, for luck; so I reckon it means that you must keep some metals *about* you."

"Yes, that must be it. It stands to reason that it is. They are in the nature of lightning-rods, you know. Put on your fireman's helmet, Mortimer; that is mostly metal."

I got it, and put it on—a very heavy and clumsy and uncomfortable thing on a hot night in a close room. Even my night-dress seemed to be more clothing than I strictly needed.

"Mortimer, I think your middle ought to be protected. Won't you buckle on your militia saber, please?"

I complied.

"Now, Mortimer, you ought to have some way to protect your feet. Do please put on your spurs."

I did it—in silence—and kept my temper as well as I could.

"Mortimer, it says, 'Das Gewitter läuten ist sehr gefährlich, weil die Glocke selbst, sowie der durch das Läuten veranlasste Luftzug and die Höhe des Thurmes den Blitz anziehen könnten.' Mortimer, does that mean that it is dangerous not to ring the church bells during a thunder-storm?"

"Yes, it seems to mean that—if that is the past participle of the nominative case singular, and I reckon it is. Yes, I think it means that on account of the height of the church tower and the absence of *Luftzug* it would be very dangerous (*sehr gefährlich*) not to ring the bells in time of a storm; and, moreover, don't you see, the very wording—"

"Never mind that, Mortimer; don't waste the precious time in talk. Get the large dinner-bell; it is right there in the hall. Quick, Mortimer, dear; we are almost safe. Oh, dear, I do believe we are going to be saved, at last!"

Our little summer establishment stands on top of a high range of hills, overlooking a valley. Several farmhouses are in our neighborhood—the nearest some three or four hundred yards away.

When I, mounted on the chair, had been clanging that dreadful bell a matter of seven or eight minutes, our shutters were suddenly torn open from without, and a brilliant bull's-eye lantern was thrust in at the window, followed by a hoarse inquiry:

"What in the nation is the matter here?"

The window was full of men's heads, and the heads were full of eyes that stared wildly at my night-dress and my warlike accoutrements.

I dropped the bell, skipped down from the chair in confusion, and said:

"There is nothing the matter, friends—only a little discomfort on account of the thunder-storm. I was trying to keep off the lightning."

"Thunder-storm? Lightning? Why, Mr. McWilliams, have you lost your mind? It is a beautiful starlight night; there has been no storm."

I looked out, and I was so astonished I could hardly speak for a while. Then I said:

"I do not understand this. We distinctly saw the glow of the flashes through the curtains and shutters, and heard the thunder."

One after another of those people lay down on the ground to laugh—and two of them died. One of the survivors remarked:

"Pity you didn't think to open your blinds and look over to the top of the hill yonder. What you heard was cannon; what you saw was the flash. You see, the telegraph brought some news, just at midnight: Garfield's nominated—and that's what's the matter!"

Yes, Mr. Twain, as I was saying in the beginning (said Mr. McWilliams), the rules for preserving people against lightning are so excellent and so innumerable that the most incomprehensible thing in the world to me is how anybody ever manages to get struck.

So saying, he gathered up his satchel and umbrella, and departed; for the train had reached his town.

1880

The McWilliamses and the Burglar Alarm

THE conversation drifted smoothly and pleasantly along from weather to crops, from crops to literature, from literature to scandal, from scandal to religion; then took a random jump, and landed on the subject of burglar alarms. And now for the first time Mr. McWilliams showed feeling. Whenever I perceive this sign on this man's dial, I comprehend it, and lapse into silence, and give him opportunity to unload his heart. Said he, with but ill-controlled emotion:

I do not go one single cent on burglar alarms, Mr. Twain—not a single cent—and I will tell you why. When we were finishing our house, we found we had a little cash left over, on account of the plumber not knowing it. I was for enlightening the heathen with it, for I was always unaccountably down on the heathen somehow; but Mrs. McWilliams said no, let's have a burglar alarm. I agreed to this compromise. I will explain that whenever I want a thing, and Mrs. McWilliams wants another thing, and we decide upon the thing that Mrs. McWilliams wants—as we always do—she calls that a compromise. Very well: the man came up from New York and put in the alarm, and charged three hundred and twenty-five dollars for it, and said we could sleep without uneasiness now. So we did for awhile—say a month. Then one night we smelled smoke, and I was advised to get up and see what the matter was. I lit a candle, and started toward the stairs, and met a burglar coming out of a room with a basket of tinware, which he had mistaken for solid silver in the dark. He was smoking a pipe. I said, "My friend, we do not allow smoking in this room." He said he was a stranger, and could not be expected to know the rules of the house: said he had been in many houses just as good as this one, and it had never been objected to before. He added that as far as his experience went, such rules had never been considered to apply to burglars, anyway.

I said: "Smoke along, then, if it is the custom, though I think that the conceding of a privilege to a burglar which is denied to a bishop is a conspicuous sign of the looseness of the times. But waiving all that, what business have you to be entering this house in this furtive and clandestine way, without ringing the burglar alarm?"

He looked confused and ashamed, and said, with embarrassment: "I beg a thousand pardons. I did not know you had a burglar alarm, else I would have rung it. I beg you will not mention it where my parents may hear of it, for they are old and feeble, and such a seemingly wanton breach of the hallowed conventionalities of our Christian civilization might all too rudely sunder the frail bridge which hangs darkling between the pale and evanescent present and the solemn great deeps of the eternities. May I trouble you for a match?"

I said: "Your sentiments do you honor, but if you will allow me to say it, metaphor is not your best hold. Spare your thigh; this kind light only on the box, and seldom there, in fact, if my experience may be trusted. But to return to business; how did you get in here?"

"Through a second-story window.

It was even so. I redeemed the tinware at pawnbroker's rates, less cost of advertising, bade the burglar good-night, closed the window after him, and retired to headquarters to report. Next morning we sent for the burglar-alarm man, and he came up and explained that the reason the alarm did not "go off" was that no part of the house but the first floor was attached to the alarm. This was simply idiotic; one might as well have no armor on at all in battle as to have it only on his legs. The expert now put the whole second story on the alarm, charged three hundred dollars for it, and went his way. By and by, one night, I found a burglar in the third story, about to start down a ladder with a lot of miscellaneous property. My first impulse was to crack his head with a billiard cue; but my second was to refrain from this attention, because he was between me and the cue rack. The second impulse was plainly the soundest, so I refrained, and proceeded to compromise. I redeemed the property at former rates, after deducting ten per cent. for use of ladder, it being my ladder, and next day we sent down for the expert once more, and had the third story attached to the alarm, for three hundred dollars.

By this time the "annunciator" had grown to formidable dimensions. It had forty-seven tags on it, marked with the names of the various rooms and chimneys, and it occupied the space of an ordinary wardrobe. The gong was the size of a wash-bowl, and was placed above the head of our bed. There was a wire from the house to the coachman's quarters in the stable, and a noble gong alongside his pillow.

We should have been comfortable now but for one defect. Every morning at five the cook opened the kitchen door, in the way of business, and rip went that gong! The first time this happened I thought the last day was come sure. I didn't think it *in* bed—no, but out of it—for the first effect of that frightful gong is to hurl you across the house, and slam you against the wall, and then curl you up, and squirm you like a spider on a stove lid, till somebody shuts the kitchen door. In solid fact, there is no clamor that is even remotely comparable to the dire clamor which that gong makes. Well, this catastrophe happened every morning regularly at five o'clock, and lost us three hours sleep; for, mind you, when that thing wakes you, it doesn't merely wake you in spots; it wakes you all over, conscience and all, and you are good for eighteen hours of wide-awakeness subsequently—eighteen hours of the very most inconceivable wide-awakeness that you ever experienced in your life. A stranger died on our hands one time, and we vacated and left him in our room overnight. Did that stranger wait for the general judgment? *No*, sir; he got up at five the next morning in the most prompt and unostentatious way. I knew he would; I knew it mighty well. He collected his life-insurance, and lived happy ever after, for there was plenty of proof as to the perfect squareness of his death.

Well, we were gradually fading toward a better land, on account of the daily loss of sleep; so we finally had the expert up again, and he ran a wire to the outside of the door, and placed a switch there, whereby Thomas, the butler, always made one little mistake—he switched the alarm off at night when he went to bed, and switched it on again at daybreak in the morning, just in time for the cook to open the kitchen door, and enable that gong to slam us across the house, sometimes breaking a window with one or the other of us. At the end of a week we recognized that this switch business was a delusion and a snare. We also discovered that a band of burglars had been lodging in the house the whole time—not exactly to steal, for there wasn't much left now, but to hide from the police. For they were hot pressed, and they shrewdly judged that the detectives would never think of a tribe of burglars taking sanctuary in a house notoriously protected by the most imposing and elaborate burglar alarm in America.

Sent down for the expert again, and this time he struck a most dazzling idea—he fixed the thing so that opening the kitchen door would take off the alarm. It was a noble idea, and he charged accordingly. But you already foresee the result. I switched on the alarm every night at bed-time, no longer trusting on Thomas's frail memory; and as soon as the lights were out the burglars walked in at the kitchen door, thus taking the alarm off without waiting for the cook to do it in the morning. You see how aggravatingly we were situated. For months we couldn't have any company. Not a spare bed in the house; all occupied by burglars.

Finally, I got up a cure of my own. The expert answered the call, and ran another ground wire to the stable, and established a switch there, so that the coachman could put on and take off the alarm. That worked first rate, and a season of peace ensued, during which we got to inviting company once more and enjoying life.

But by and by the irrepressible alarm invented a new kink. One winter's night we were flung out of bed by the sudden music of that awful gong, and when we hobbled to the annunciator, turned up the gas, and saw the word "Nursery" exposed, Mrs. McWilliams fainted dead away, and I came precious near doing the same thing myself. I seized my shotgun, and stood timing the coachman whilst that appalling buzzing went on. I knew that his gong had flung him out, too, and that he would be along with his gun as soon as he could jump into his clothes. When I judged that the time was ripe, I crept to the room next the nursery, glanced through the window, and saw the dim outline of the coachman in the yard below, standing at present-arms and waiting for a chance. Then I hopped into the nursery and fired, and in the same instant the coachman fired at the red flash of my gun. Both of us were successful; I crippled a nurse, and he shot off all my back hair. We turned up the gas, and telephoned for a surgeon. There was not a sign of a burglar, and no window had been raised. One glass was absent, but that was where the coachman's charge had come through. Here was a fine mystery—a burglar alarm "going off" at midnight of its own accord, and not a burglar in the neighborhood!

The expert answered the usual call, and explained that it was a "False alarm." Said it was easily fixed. So he overhauled the nursery window, charged a remunerative figure for it, and departed.

What we suffered from false alarms for the next three years no stylographic pen can describe. During the next three months I always flew with my gun to the room indicated, and the coachman always sallied forth with his battery to support me. But there was never anything to shoot at—windows all tight and secure. We always sent down for the expert next day, and he fixed those particular windows so they would keep quiet a week or so, and always remembered to send us a bill about like this:

Wire	$2.15
Nipple	.75
Two hours' labor	1.50
Wax	.47
Tape	.34
Screws	.15
Recharging battery	.98
Three hours' labor	2.25
String	.02
Lard	.66
Pond's Extract	1.25
Springs at 50	2.00
Railroad fares	7.25
	$19.77

At length a perfectly natural thing came about—after we had answered three or four hundred false alarms—to wit, we stopped answering them. Yes, I simply rose up calmly, when slammed across the house by the alarm, calmly inspected the annunciator, took note of the room indicated, and then calmly disconnected that room from the alarm, and went back to bed as if nothing had happened. Moreover, I left that room off permanently, and did not send for the expert. Well, it goes without saying that in the course of time *all* the rooms were taken off, and the entire machine was out of service.

It was at this unprotected time that the heaviest calamity of all happened. The burglars walked in one night and carried off the burglar alarm! yes, sir, every hide and hair of it: ripped it out, tooth and nail; springs, bells, gongs, battery, and all; they took a hundred and fifty miles of copper wire; they just cleaned her out, bag and baggage, and never left us a vestige of her to swear at—swear by, I mean.

We had a time of it to get her back; but we accomplished it finally, for money. The alarm firm said that what we needed now was to have her put in right—with their new patent springs in the windows to make false alarms impossible, and their new patent clock attached to take off and put on the alarm morning and night without human assistance. That seemed a good scheme. They promised to have the whole thing finished in ten days. They began work, and we left for the summer. They worked a couple of days; then *they* left for the summer. After which the burglars moved in, and began *their* summer vacation. When we returned in the fall, the house was as empty as a beer closet in premises where painters have been at work. We refurnished, and then sent down to hurry up the expert. He came up and finished the job, and said: "Now this clock is set to put on the alarm every night at 10, and take it off every morning at 5:45. All you've got to do is to wind her up every week, and then leave her alone—she will take care of the alarm herself."

After that we had a most tranquil season during three

months. The bill was prodigious, of course, and I had said I would not pay it until the new machinery had proved itself to be flawless. The time stipulated was three months. So I paid the bill, and the very next day the alarm went to buzzing like ten thousand bee swarms at ten o'clock in the morning. I turned the hands around twelve hours, according to instructions, and this took off the alarm; but there was another hitch at night, and I had to set her ahead twelve hours once more to get her to put the alarm on again. That sort of nonsense went on a week or two, then the expert came up and put in a new clock. He came up every three months during the next three years, and put in a new clock. But it was always a failure. His clocks all had the same perverse defect: they would put the alarm on in the daytime, and they would *not* put it on at night; and if you forced it on yourself, they *would* take it off again the minute your back was turned.

Now there is the history of that burglar alarm—everything just as it happened; nothing extenuated, and naught set down in malice. Yes, sir,—and when I had slept nine years with burglars, and maintained an expensive burglar alarm the whole time, for their protection, not mine, and at my sole cost—for not a d—d cent could I ever get *them* to contribute—I just said to Mrs. McWilliams that I had had enough of that kind of pie; so with her full consent I took the whole thing out and traded it off for a dog, and shot the dog. I don't know what *you* think about it, Mr. Twain; but *I* think those things are made solely in the interest of the burglars. Yes, sir, a burglar alarm combines in its person all that is objectionable about a fire, a riot, and a harem, and at the same time had none of the compensating advantages, of one sort or another, that customarily belong with that combination. Good-by: I get off here.

1882

Extracts from Adam's Diary

MONDAY.—This new creature with the long hair is a good deal in the way. It is always hanging around and following me about. I don't like this; I am not used to company. I wish it would stay with the other animals...Cloudy to-day, wind in the east; think we shall have rain...*We?* Where did I get that word?—I remember now—the new creature uses it.

Tuesday.—Been examining the great waterfall. It is the finest thing on the estate, I think. The new creature calls it Niagara Falls—why, I am sure I do not know. Says it *looks* like Niagara Falls. That is not a reason, it is mere waywardness and imbecility. I get no chance to name anything myself. The new creature names everything that comes along, before I can get in a protest. And always that same pretext is offered—it *looks* like the thing. There is the dodo, for instance. Says the moment one looks at it one sees at a glance that it "looks like a dodo." It will have to keep that name, no doubt. It wearies me to fret about it, and it does no good, anyway. Dodo! It looks no more like a dodo than I do.

Wednesday.—Built me a shelter against the rain, but could not have it to myself in peace. The new creature intruded. When I tried to put it out it shed water out of the holes it looks with, and wiped it away with the back of its paws, and made a noise such as some of the other animals make when they are in distress. I wish it would not talk; it is always talking. That sounds like a cheap fling at the poor creature, a slur; but I do not mean it so. I have never heard the human voice before, and any new and strange sound intruding itself here upon the solemn hush of these dreaming solitudes offends my ear and seems a false note. And this new sound is so close to me; it is right at my shoulder, right at my ear, first on one side and then on the other, and I am used only to sounds that are more or less distant from me.

Friday.—The naming goes recklessly on, in spite of anything I can do. I had a very good name for the estate, and it was musical and pretty—GARDEN OF EDEN. Privately, I continue to call it that, but not any longer publicly. The new creature says it is all woods and rocks and scenery, and therefore has no resemblance to a garden. Says it *looks* like a park, and does not look like anything *but* a park. Consequently, without consulting me, it has been new-named—NIAGARA FALLS PARK. This is sufficiently high-handed, it seems to me. And already there is a sign up:

KEEP OFF
THE GRASS

My life is not as happy as it was.

Saturday.—The new creature eats too much fruit. We are going to run short, most likely. "We" again—that is *its* word; mine, too, now, from hearing it so much. Good deal of fog this morning. I do not go out in the fog myself. The new creature does. It goes out in all weathers, and stumps right in with its muddy feet. And talks. It used to be so pleasant and quiet here.

Sunday.—Pulled through. This day is getting to be more and more trying. It was selected and set apart last November as a day of rest. I had already six of them per week before. This morning found the new creature trying to clod apples out of that forbidden tree.

Monday.—The new creature says its name is Eve. That is all right, I have no objections. Says it is to call it by, when I want it to come. I said it was superfluous, then. The word evidently raised me in its respect; and indeed it is a large, good word and will bear repetition. It says it is not an It, it is a She. This is probably doubtful; yet it is all one to me; what she is were nothing to me if she would but go by herself and not talk.

Tuesday.—She has littered the whole estate with execrable names and offensive signs:

THIS WAY TO THE WHIRLPOOL
THIS WAY TO GOAT ISLAND
CAVE OF THE WINDS THIS WAY

She says this park would make a tidy summer resort if there was any custom for it. Summer resort—another invention of hers—just words, without any meaning. What is a summer resort? But it is best not to ask her, she has such a rage for explaining.

Friday.—She has taken to beseeching me to stop going over the Falls. What harm does it do? Says it makes her shudder. I wonder why; I have always done it—always liked the plunge, and coolness. I supposed it was what the Falls were for. They have no other use that

I can see, and they must have been made for something. She says they were only made for scenery—like the rhinoceros and the mastodon.

I went over the Falls in a barrel—not satisfactory to her. Went over in a tub—still not satisfactory. Swam the Whirlpool and the Rapids in a fig-leaf suit. It got much damaged. Hence, tedious complaints about my extravagance. I am too much hampered here. What I need is change of scene.

Saturday.—I escaped last Tuesday night, and traveled two days, and built me another shelter in a secluded place, and obliterated my tracks as well as I could, but she hunted me out by means of a beast which she has tamed and calls a wolf, and came making that pitiful noise again, and shedding that water out of the places she looks with. I was obliged to return with her, but will presently emigrate again when occasion offers. She engages herself in many foolish things; among others, to study out why the animals called lions and tigers live on grass and flowers, when, as she says, the sort of teeth they wear would indicate that they were intended to eat each other. This is foolish, because to do that would be to kill each other, and that would introduce what, as I understand it, is called "death"; and death, as I have been told, has not yet entered the Park. Which is a pity, on some accounts.

Sunday.—Pulled through.

Monday.—I believe I see what the week is for: it is to give time to rest up from the weariness of Sunday. It seems a good idea...She has been climbing that tree again. Clodded her out of it. She said nobody was looking. Seems to consider that a sufficient justification for chancing any dangerous thing. Told her that. The word justification moved her admiration—and envy, too, I thought. It is a good word.

Tuesday.—She told me she was made out of a rib taken from my body. This is at least doubtful, if not more than that. I have not missed any rib.... She is in much trouble about the buzzard; says grass does not agree with it; is afraid she can't raise it; thinks it was intended to live on decayed flesh. The buzzard must get along the best it can with what it is provided. We cannot overturn the whole scheme to accommodate the buzzard.

Saturday.—She fell in the pond yesterday when she was looking at herself in it, which she is always doing. She nearly strangled, and said it was most uncomfortable. This made her sorry for the creatures which live in there, which she calls fish, for she continues to fasten names on to things that don't need them and don't come when they are called by them, which is a matter of no consequence to her, she is such a numskull, anyway; so she got a lot of them out and brought them in last night and put them in my bed to keep warm, but I have noticed them now and then all day and I don't see that they are any happier there then they were before, only quieter. When night comes I shall throw them outdoors. I will not sleep with them again, for I find them clammy and unpleasant to lie among when a person hasn't anything on.

Sunday.—Pulled through.

Tuesday.—She has taken up with a snake now. The other animals are glad, for she was always experimenting with them and bothering them; and I am glad because the snake talks, and this enables me to get a rest.

Friday.—She says the snake advises her to try the fruit of that tree, and says the result will be a great and fine and noble education. I told her there would be another result, too—it would introduce death into the world. That was a mistake—it had been better to keep the remark to myself; it only gave her an idea—she could save the sick buzzard, and furnish fresh meat to the despondent lions and tigers. I advised her to keep away from the tree. She said she wouldn't. I foresee trouble. Will emigrate.

Wednesday.—I have had a variegated time. I escaped last night, and rode a horse all night as fast as he could go, hoping to get clear out of the Park and hide some other country before the trouble should begin; but it was not to be. About an hour after sun-up, as I was riding through a flowery plain where thousands of animals were grazing, slumbering, or playing with each other, according to their wont, all of a sudden they broke into a tempest of frightful noises, and in one moment the plain was a frantic commotion and every beast was destroying its neighbor. I knew what it meant—Eve had eaten that fruit, and death was come into the world.... The tigers ate my horse, paying no attention when I ordered them to desist, and they would have eaten me if I had stayed—which I didn't, but went away in much haste.... I found this place, outside the Park, and was fairly comfortable for a few days, but she has found me out. Found me out, and has named the place Tonawanda—says it *looks* like that. In fact I was not sorry she came, for there are but meager pickings here, and she brought some of those apples. I was obliged to eat them, I was so hungry. It was against my principles, but I find that principles have no real force except when one is well fed.... She came curtained in boughs and bunches of leaves, and when I asked her what she meant by such nonsense, and snatched them away and threw them down, she tittered and blushed. I had never seen a person titter and blush before, and to me it seemed unbecoming and idiotic. She said I would soon know how it was myself. This was correct. Hungry as I was, I laid down the apple half-eaten—certainly the best one I ever saw, considering the lateness of the season—and arrayed myself in the discarded boughs and branches, and then spoke to her with some severity and ordered her to go and get some more and not make such a spectacle of herself. She did it, and after this we crept down to where the wild-beast battle had been, and collected some skins, and I made her patch together a couple of suits proper for public occasions. They are uncomfortable, it is true, but stylish, and that is the main point about clothes.... I find she is a good deal of a companion. I see I should be lonesome and depressed without her, now that I have lost my property. Another thing, she says it is ordered that we work for our living hereafter. She will be useful. I will superintend.

Ten Days Later.—She accuses *me* of being the cause of our disaster! She says, with apparent sincerity and truth, that the Serpent assured her that the forbidden fruit was not apples, it was chestnuts. I said I was innocent, then, for I had not eaten any chestnuts. She said the Serpent informed her that "chestnut" was a figurative term meaning an aged and moldy joke. I turned pale at that, for I have made many jokes to pass the weary time, and some of them could have been of that sort, though I had honestly supposed that they were new when I made them. She asked me if I had made one just at the time of the catastrophe. I was obliged to admit that I had made one to myself, though not aloud. It was this. I was thinking about the Falls, and I said to myself, "How wonderful it is to see that vast body of water tumble down there!" Then in an instant a bright thought flashed into my head, and I let it fly, saying, "It would be a deal more wonderful to see it tumble *up* there!"—and I was just about to kill myself with laughing at it when all nature broke loose in war and death and I had to flee for my life. "There," she said, with triumph, "that is just it; the Serpent mentioned that very jest, and called it the First Chestnut, and said it was coeval with the creation." Alas, I am indeed to blame. Would that I were not witty; oh, that I had never had that radiant thought!

Next Year.—We have named it Cain. She caught it while I was up country trapping on the North Shore of the Erie; caught it in the timber a couple of miles from our dug-out—or it might have been four, she isn't certain which. It resembles us in some ways, and may be a relation. That is what she thinks, but this is an error, in my judgment. The difference in size warrants the conclusion that it is a different and new kind of animal—a fish, perhaps, though when I put it in the water to see, it sank, and she plunged in and snatched it out before there was opportunity for the experiment to determine the matter. I still think it is a fish, but she is indifferent about what it is, and will not let me have it to try. I do not understand this. The coming of the creature seems to have changed her whole nature and made her unreasonable about experiments. She thinks more of it than she does of any of the other animals, but is not able to explain why. Her mind is disordered—everything shows it. Sometimes she carries the fish in her arms half the night when it complains and wants to get to the water. At such times the water comes out of the places in her face that she looks out of, and she pats the fish on the back and makes soft sounds with her mouth to soothe it, and betrays sorrow and solicitude in a hundred ways. I have never seen her do like this with any other fish, and it troubles me greatly. She used to carry the young tigers around so, and play with them, before we lost our property, but it was only play; she never took on about them like this when their dinner disagreed with them.

Sunday.—She doesn't work, Sundays, but lies around all tired out, and likes to have the fish wallow over her; and she makes fool noises to amuse it, and pretends to chew its paws, and that makes it laugh. I have not seen a fish before that could laugh. This makes me doubt.... I have come to like Sunday myself. Superintending all the week tires a body so. There ought to be more Sundays. In the old days they were tough, but now they come handy.

Wednesday.—It isn't a fish. I cannot quite make out what it is. It makes curious devilish noises when not satisfied, and says "goo-goo" when it is. It is not one of us, for it doesn't walk; it is not a bird, for it doesn't fly; it is not a frog, for it doesn't hop; it is not a snake, for it doesn't crawl. I feel sure it is not a fish, though I cannot get a chance to find out whether it can swim or not. It merely lies around, and mostly on its back, with its feet up. I have not seen any other animal do that before. I said I believed it was an enigma; but she only admired the word without understanding it. In my judgment it is either an enigma or some kind of a bug. If it dies, I will take it apart and see what its arrangements are. I never had a thing perplex me so.

Three Months Later.—The perplexity augments instead of diminishing. I sleep but little. It has ceased from lying around, and goes about on its four legs now. Yet it differs from the other four-legged animals, in that its front legs are unusually short, consequently this causes the main part of its person to stick up uncomfortably high in the air, and this is not attractive. It is built much as we are, but its method of traveling shows that it is not of our breed. The short front legs and long hind ones indicate that it is of the kangaroo family, but it is a marked variation of the species, since the true kangaroo hops, whereas this one never does. Still it is a curious and interesting variety, and has not been catalogued before. As I discovered it, I have felt justified in securing the credit of the discovery by attaching my name to it, and hence have called it *Kangaroorum Adamiensis*.... It must have been a young one when it came, for it has grown exceedingly since. It must be five times as big, now, as it was then, and when discontented it is able to make from twenty-two to thirty-eight times the noise it made at first. Coercion does not modify this, but has the contrary effect. For this reason I discontinued the system. She reconciles it by persuasion, and by giving it things which she had previously told me she wouldn't give it. As already observed, I was not at home when it first came, and she told me she found it in the woods. It seems odd that it should be the only one, yet it must be so, for I have worn myself out these many weeks trying to find another one to add to my collection, and for this one to play with; for surely then it would be quieter and we could tame it more easily. But I find none, nor any vestige of any; and strangest of all, no tracks. It has to live on the ground, it cannot help itself; therefore, how does it get about without leaving a track? I have set a dozen traps, but they do no good. I catch all small animals except that one; animals that merely go into the trap out of curiosity, I think, to see what the milk is there for. They never drink it.

Three Months Later.—The Kangaroo still continues to grow, which is very strange and perplexing. I never knew one to be so long getting its growth. It has fur on its head now; not like kangaroo fur, but exactly like our hair except that it is much finer and softer, and instead of being black is red. I am like to lose my mind over the capricious and harassing developments of this unclassifiable zoological freak. If I could catch another one—but that is hopeless; it is a new variety, and the only sample; this is plain. But I caught a true kangaroo and brought it in, thinking that this one, being lonesome, would rather have that for company than have no kin at all, or any animal it could feel a nearness to or get sympathy from in its forlorn condition here among strangers who do not know its ways or habits, or what to do to make it feel that it is among friends; but it was a mistake—it went into such fits at the sight of the kangaroo that I was convinced it had never seen one before. I pity the poor noisy little animal, but there is nothing I can do to make it happy. If I could tame it—but that is out of the question; the more I try the worse I seem to make it. It grieves me to the heart to see it in its little storms of sorrow and passion. I wanted to let it go, but she wouldn't hear of it. That seemed cruel and not like her; and yet she may be right. It might be lonelier than ever; for since I cannot find another one, how could it?

Five Months Later.—It is not a kangaroo. No, for it supports itself by holding to her finger, and thus goes a few steps on its hind legs, and then falls down. It is probably some kind of a bear; and yet it has no tail—as yet—and no fur, except on its head. It still keeps on growing—that is a curious circumstance, for bears get their growth earlier than this. Bears are dangerous—since our catastrophe—and I shall not be satisfied to have this one prowling about the place much longer without a muzzle on. I have offered to get her a kangaroo if she would let this one go, but it did no good—she is determined to run us into all sorts of foolish risks, I think. She was not like this before she lost her mind.

A Fortnight Later.—I examined its mouth. There is no danger yet: it has only one tooth. It has no tail yet. It makes more noise now than it ever did before—and mainly at night. I have moved out. But I shall go over, mornings, to breakfast, and see if it has more teeth. If it gets a mouthful of teeth it will be time for it to go, tail or no tail, for a bear does not need a tail in order to be dangerous.

Four Months Later.—I have been off hunting and fishing a month, up in the region that she calls Buffalo; I don't know why, unless it is because there are not any buffaloes there. Meantime the bear has learned to paddle around all by itself on its hind legs, and says "poppa" and "momma." It is certainly a new species. This resemblance to words may be purely accidental, of course, and may have no purpose or meaning; but even in that case it is still extraordinary, and is a thing which no other bear can do. This imitation of speech, taken together with general absence of fur and entire absence of tail, sufficiently indicates that this is a new kind of bear. The further study of it will be exceedingly interesting. Meantime I will go off on a far expedition among the forests of the north and make an exhaustive search. There must certainly be another one somewhere, and this one will be less dangerous when it has company of its own species. I will go straightway; but I will muzzle this one first.

Three Months Later.—It has been a weary, weary hunt, yet I have had no success. In the mean time, without stirring from the home estate, she has caught another one! I never saw such luck. I might have hunted these woods a hundred years, I never would have run across that thing.

Next Day.—I have been comparing the new one with the old one, and it is perfectly plain that they are the same breed. I was going to stuff one of them for my collection, but she is prejudiced against it for some reason or other; so I have relinquished the idea, though I think it is a mistake. It would be an irreparable loss to science if they should get away. The old one is tamer than it was and can laugh and talk like the parrot, having learned this, no doubt, from being with the parrot so much, and having the imitative faculty in a highly developed degree. I shall be astonished if it turns out to be a new kind of parrot; and yet I ought not to be astonished, for it has already been everything else it could think of since those first days when it was a fish. The new one is as ugly now as the old one was at first; has the same sulphur-and-raw-meat complexion and the same singular head without any fur on it. She calls it Abel.

Ten Years Later.—They are *boys*; we found it out long ago. It was their coming in that small, immature shape that puzzled us; we were not used to it. There are some girls now. Abel is a good boy, but if Cain had stayed a bear it would have improved him. After all these years, I see that I was mistaken about Eve in the beginning; it is better to live outside the Garden with her than inside it without her. At first I thought she talked too much; but now I should be sorry to have that voice fall silent and pass out of my life. Blessed be the chestnut that brought us near together and taught me to know the goodness of her heart and the sweetness of her spirit!

1893

How to Tell a Story

THE HUMOROUS STORY
AN AMERICAN DEVELOPMENT.—
ITS DIFFERENCE FROM COMIC AND WITTY STORIES

I DO not claim that I can tell a story as it ought to be told. I only claim to know how a story ought to be told, for I have been almost daily in the company of the most expert story-tellers for many years.

There are several kinds of stories, but only one difficult kind—the humorous. I will talk mainly about that one. The humorous story is American, the comic story is English, the witty story is French. The humorous story depends for its effect upon the *manner* of the telling; the comic story and the witty story upon the *matter*.

The humorous story may be spun out to great length, and may wander around as much as it pleases, and arrive nowhere in particular; but the comic and witty stories must be brief and end with a point. The humorous story bubbles gently along, the others burst.

The humorous story is strictly a work of art—high and delicate art—and only an artist can tell it; but no art is necessary in telling the comic and the witty story; anybody can do it. The art of telling a humorous story —understand, I mean by word of mouth, not print— was created in America, and has remained at home.

The humorous story is told gravely; the teller does his best to conceal the fact that he even dimly suspects that there is anything funny about it; but the teller of the comic story tells you beforehand that it is one of the funniest things he has ever heard, then tells it with eager delight, and is the first person to laugh when he gets through. And sometimes, if he has had good success, he is so glad and happy that he will repeat the "nub" of it and glance around from face to face, collecting applause, and then repeat it again. It is a pathetic thing to see.

Very often, of course, the rambling and disjointed humorous story finishes with a nub, point, snapper, or whatever you like to call it. Then the listener must be alert, for in many cases the teller will divert attention from that nub by dropping it in a carefully casual and indifferent way, with the pretense that he does not know it is a nub.

Artemus Ward used that trick a good deal; then when the belated audience presently caught the joke he would look up with innocent surprise, as if wondering what they had found to laugh at. Dan Setchell used it before him, Nye and Riley and others use it to-day.

But the teller of the comic story does not slur the nub; he shouts it at you—every time. And when he prints it, in England, France, Germany, and Italy, he italicizes it, puts some whooping exclamation-points after it, and sometimes explains it in a parenthesis. All of which is very depressing, and makes one want to renounce joking and lead a better life.

Let me set down an instance of the comic method, using an anecdote which has been popular all over the world for twelve or fifteen hundred years. The teller tells it in this way:

THE WOUNDED SOLDIER

In the course of a certain battle a soldier whose leg had been shot off appealed to another soldier who was hurrying by to carry him to the rear, informing him at the same time of the loss which he had sustained; whereupon the generous son of Mars, shouldering the unfortunate, proceeded to carry out his desire. The bullets and cannon-balls were flying in all directions, and presently one of the latter took the wounded man's head off—without, however, his deliverer being aware of it. In no long time he was hailed by an officer, who said:

"Where are you going with that carcass?"

"To the rear, sir—he's lost his leg!"

"His leg, forsooth?" responded the astonished officer; "you mean his head, you booby."

Whereupon the soldier dispossessed himself of his burden, and stood looking down upon it in great perplexity. At length he said:

"It is true, sir, just as you have said." Then after a pause he added, "*But he* TOLD *me* IT WAS HIS LEG!!!!!"

Here the narrator bursts into explosion after explosion of thunderous horse-laughter, repeating that nub from time to time through his gaspings and shriekings and suffocatings.

It takes only a minute and a half to tell that in its comic-story form; and isn't worth the telling, after all. Put into the humorous-story form it takes ten minutes, and is about the funniest thing I have ever listened to—as James Whitcomb Riley tells it.

He tells it in the character of a dull-witted old farmer

who has just heard it for the first time, thinks it is unspeakably funny, and is trying to repeat it to a neighbor. But he can't remember it; so he gets all mixed up and wanders helplessly round and round, putting in tedious details that don't belong in the tale and only retard it; taking them out conscientiously and putting in others that are just as useless; making minor mistakes now and then and stopping to correct them and explain how he came to make them; remembering things which he forgot to put in in their proper place and going back to put them in there; stopping his narrative a good while in order to try to recall the name of the soldier that was hurt, and finally remembering that the soldier's name was not mentioned, and remarking placidly that the name is of no real importance, anyway—better, of course, if one knew it, but not essential, after all—and so on, and so on, and so on.

The teller is innocent and happy and pleased with himself, and has to stop every little while to hold himself in and keep from laughing outright; and does hold in, but his body quakes in a jelly-like way with interior chuckles; and at the end of the ten minutes the audience have laughed until they are exhausted, and the tears are running down their faces.

The simplicity and innocence and sincerity and unconsciousness of the old farmer are perfectly simulated, and the result is a performance which is thoroughly charming and delicious. This is art—and fine and beautiful, and only a master can compass it; but a machine could tell the other story.

To string incongruities and absurdities together in a wandering and sometimes purposeless way, and seem innocently unaware that they are absurdities, is the basis of the American art, if my position is correct. Another feature is the slurring of the point. A third is the dropping of a studied remark apparently without knowing it, as if one were thinking aloud. The fourth and last is the pause.

Artemus Ward dealt in numbers three and four a good deal. He would begin to tell with great animation something which he seemed to think was wonderful; then lose confidence, and after an apparently absent-minded pause add an incongruous remark in a soliloquizing way; and that was the remark intended to explode the mine—and it did.

For instance, he would say eagerly, excitedly, "I once knew a man in New Zealand who hadn't a tooth in his head"—here his animation would die out; a silent, reflective pause would follow, then he would say dreamily, and as if to himself, "and yet that man could beat a drum better than any man I ever saw."

The pause is an exceedingly important feature in any kind of story, and a frequently recurring feature, too. It is a dainty thing, and delicate, and also uncertain and treacherous; for it must be exactly the right length—no more and no less—or it fails of its purpose and makes trouble. If the pause is too short the impressive point is passed, and the audience have had time to divine that a surprise is intended—and then you can't surprise them, of course.

On the platform I used to tell a negro ghost story that had a pause in front of the snapper on the end, and that pause was the most important thing in the whole story. If I got it the right length precisely, I could spring the finishing ejaculation with effect enough to make some impressible girl deliver a startled little yelp and jump out of her seat—and that was what I was after. This story was called "The Golden Arm," and was told in this fashion. You can practise with it yourself—and mind you look out for the pause and get it right.

THE GOLDEN ARM

Once 'pon a time dey wuz a monsus mean man, en he live way out in de prairie all 'lone by hisself, 'cep'n he had a wife. En bimeby she died, en he tuck en toted her way out dah in de prairie en buried her. Well, she had a golden arm—all solid gold, fum de shoulder down. He wiz pow'ful mean—pow'ful; en dat night he couldn't sleep, caze he want dat golden arm so bad.

When it come midnight he couldn't stan' it no mo'; so he git up, he did, en tuck his lantern en shoved out thoo de storm en dug her up en got de golden arm; en he bent his head down 'gin de win', en plowed en plowed en plowed thoo de snow. Den all on a sudden he stop (make a considerable pause here, and look startled, and take a listening attitude) en say: "My *lan'*, what's dat?"

En he listen—en listen—en de win' say (set your teeth together and imitate the wailing and wheezing singsong of the wind), "Buzzz-z-zzz"—en den, way back yonder whah de grave is, he hear a *voice!*—he hear a voice all mix' up in de win' can't hardly tell 'em 'part— "Buzz—zzz—W-h-o—g-o-t—m-y—g-o-l-d-e-n —*arm?*" (You must begin to shiver violently now.)

En he begin to shiver en shake, en say, "Oh, my! *Oh*, my lan'!" en de win' blow de lantern out, en de snow en sleet blow in his face en most' choke him, en he start aplowin' knee-deep towards home mos' dead, he so sk'yerd—en pooty soon he hear de voice agin, en (pause) it 'us comin *after* him! "Bzzz—zzzzzz—W-h-o—g-o-t —m-y—g-o-l-d-e-n—*arm?*"

When he git to de pasture he hear it again—closter now, en a-*comin'!*—a-comin' back dah in de dark en de storm—(repeat the wind and the voice). When he git to de house he rush up-stairs en jump in de bed en kiver up, head and years, en lay dah shiverin' en shakin'—en den way out dah he hear it *agin!*—en a-*comin'!* En bimeby he hear (pause—awed, listening attitude)—pat—pat—pat—*hit's a-comin' up-stairs!* Den he hear de latch, en he *know* it's in de room!

Den pooty soon he know it's a-*stannin' by de bed!* (Pause.) Den—he know it's a-*bendin' down over him*—en he cain't skasely git his breath! Den—den—he seem to feel someth'n' *c-o-l-d*, right down 'most agin his head! (Pause.)

Den de voice say, *right at his year*— "*W-h-o—g-o-t—m-y—g-o-l-d-e-n arm?*" (You must wail it out very plaintively and accusingly); then you stare steadily and impressively into the face of the farthest-gone auditor—a girl, preferably—and let that awe-inspiring pause begin to build itself in the deep hush. When it has reached exactly the right length, jump suddenly at that girl and yell, "*You've* got it!"

If you've got the *pause* right, she'll fetch a dear little yelp and spring right out of her shoes. But you *must* get the pause right; and you will find it the most troublesome and aggravating and uncertain thing you ever undertook.

1895